CW00524235

Published by Quinn Loftis Books LLC

Dedication

To all the readers who have stuck with this series for eight and a half books!

Acknowledgments

As usual there are many people to thank when it comes to finishing a book. Thank you to God, first and foremost, for blessing me and for loving me. Thank you to my husband for being so very understanding, patient and helpful. I couldn't do this without you and I'm so thankful that you are mine. Thank you to my son Travis for his patience with me for all the times I've had to say *I'm writing right now, buddy.* You are truly one of a kind and I'm blessed to get to be your mother. Thank you to Candace Selph for being a great PA, an amazing friend and sister in Christ. Your opinion and input is invaluable to me. Thank you to Kelli Cole, the greatest nanny ever and an amazing friend. I truly appreciate your encouragement and help, there are many days I wouldn't have been able to get any writing done had you not been there. Thank you to everyone who has put up with me throughout this pregnancy, while I wrote a book about a pregnant character. I know I've been a total pain, and frankly I've gotten on my own nerves. I truly am thankful for so many people who love me through the difficult times.

Chapter 1

"MAKE IT STOP! FANE, PLEASE MAKE IT STOP!" Jacquelyn's cries pierced to the deepest part of his soul. Fane stood frozen, staring at his mate, unable to move any closer to her as she reached for him and begged him to make it—make *them*— stop. His heart was being squeezed by an invisible fist as his stomach threatened to crawl out of his throat. How could it be happening again? Hadn't they been rescued from the In-Between? How had he managed to find himself deep in the bowels of hell once more unable to save his mate?

"Fane." A soft voice reached into his mind attempting to block out the screams of agony.

"Fane. Wake up, wolf-man. Wake up and come back to me."

He fought for the consciousness that his mind so desperately needed in order to escape the memories, and if it wasn't for her— Jacquelyn, his mate, his love—he would be lost to them.. Only her voice, only her touch, or only her soul could soothe the wounds that just kept coming back.

His eyes slowly began to open and it took a moment until his vision was clear and he could see her face—her unmarred, tear free, beautiful face—staring down at him. The room was dark around them with only the soft glow of the moonlight reaching through the window. It lit up Jacquelyn's hair in a soft fiery glow, as though a halo of flames framed her features.

"Are you back with me?" she asked softly as she picked up his hand and pressed it to her cheek. She was warm and full of life, and not just her own.

"Did I hurt you?" he asked as he took his free hand and pressed it to her stomach. Now in her second trimester, she was finally beginning to show signs, more than just nausea, that she carried their child.

"You weren't moving this time, just growling." Jacquelyn smiled down at him as if he were her world and not her unbalanced mate that was, once again, slowly coming undone.

"I need to speak with my father." Fane pressed a kiss to her lips and gently laid her to the side as he got up from their bed. He knew it was still hours until daylight, but this couldn't wait. For a time he had gotten better. Jacquelyn's light seemed to be able to keep the darkness from consuming him, but gradually, over the past few months, it had slowly begun to return. He slipped on a pair of jeans and a t-shirt and glanced back over his shoulder at his mate. Jacque didn't move; she only stared after him. There was no condemnation in her gaze only complete adoration.

"I'll be waiting for you," she told him with a patient smile. "Just remember I'm here if you need me."

"I always need you, Luna. I just—" he paused.

She shook her head. "Don't worry about me, or us. As long as you keep the lines of communication open, we're fine. Go talk to your father; see if he can help banish your demons."

As he walked the long hall toward his Alpha's room, Fane tried to figure out what exactly was causing all of the turmoil. "Demons is right," he muttered under his breath when he could not pinpoint any one thing that could be triggering the nightmares. He thought he'd let it all go: the pain, horror, and fear of all that he'd seen. He'd thought the torture that Desdemona had inflicted upon him had died right along with her. He had been wrong.

Once he reached his parents' door he paused and raised his hand to knock. But before he could, Fane heard his father's voice.

"It's unlocked, Fane. Come in."

Fane pushed the door open and found his father sitting on a large couch in front of the fireplace, though no flames danced in its depths. He glanced toward his parents' bed and saw a large hanging curtain drawn shut separating the room.

"She's still sleeping," Vasile said softly as he motioned for him to sit.

"Did you know I was coming?" Fane asked. He took the seat to the left of his father, though he didn't sit back and get comfortable. He sat perched on the edge with his elbows resting on his knees.

"I woke feeling a disturbance in the pack bonds. It's hard to go back to sleep when that happens. I had a feeling it was you," he answered honestly. "Are things with you and Jacque alright?"

Fane rubbed his hands together roughly as he nodded. "We're fine, better than fine, actually. Except for the nightmares."

"They're back." Vasile didn't voice it as a question.

"It is as real to me as if I was still there," Fane admitted. "The smells, the sounds, and even the things I touch seem real. I honestly don't know if I would be able to wake from it without her help."

Vasile's lips turned up in an understanding smile. "True mates, they are an amazing blessing. We need them more than we realize."

"Is this to be my life now? Am I to be forever traumatized by something the other males have been able to move past? What kind of leader will I be if I can't vanquish a memory?"

Vasile leaned forward, mimicking his son's pose. His eyes narrowed as his face grew taunt. "Memories, especially painful ones, are often more difficult to defeat than a living, breathing foe standing before you. A foe cannot seep into the depths of your mind and poison you by replaying the slight over and over. It's like riding a Ferris wheel that never stops, but only gets faster and faster. With each rotation, you get sicker and sicker. It does not make you weak, Fane. It simply makes you a man. We are not gods, though we are blessed with long life. We are neither all-knowing nor infallible. We are but mere men, with a beast living inside of us. And so it is not just the man that has to defeat the memories, it is the wolf as well.

"The fact that you are seeking out help tells me you will be a great leader. A wise man never tries to do on his own what he can instead do with the help of those who love him and want to see him succeed."

Fane held his father's stare for three heartbeats before finally dropping his eyes. The words his Alpha spoke were true, he knew that, and yet it didn't give Fane the power to release whatever it was he was holding onto.

"How is my grandchild doing? Growing big and strong and driving his mother crazy already?" Vasile's voice had lost its edge and instead was full of playful mischief.

"You do realize that she hasn't given birth to him yet, right?" Fane asked with a small smile of his own. Talking about his pup was one of the few things that could put a smile on his face as of late.

"Yes, yes." Vasile waved absently. "But that doesn't mean he isn't giving her hell while still cooking."

Fane chuckled. "You are so sure it is a boy, and yes he, or she, does keep Jacquelyn on her toes with all the kicking and squirming."

"It's a boy." Vasile nodded firmly. "A grandfather just knows these things."

Fane let out a deep breath as he stood. "Whatever you say, Da." He headed for the door but stopped midway and turned back to Vasile. "Thank you, for listening."

Vasile bowed his head once. "You are much loved, Prince of Wolves, mate to Jacquelyn, son of mine. Whatever it is that wants to have you cannot, not any part of you—mind, body, or soul—because you are mine. You are pack. You are Jacque's and none of us share very well."

***

"How do you think Sally is doing?" Jen asked Jacque as she sat in the floor dangling a rattle in front of Thia who was cooing at her mother like she was the best thing since sliced bread.

"Well, it's been three months since she headed off on her mission with Peri and two weeks since we've received any texts…but we haven't gotten her back in a body bag either," Jacque replied from her lazy sprawl on the couch. "So I guess that's a positive sign."

She and Jen were doing one of their weekly, okay daily, play dates. Decebel continually gave them a hard time about it because he claimed the play dates were supposed to be for children. Jen happily informed him that play dates were also for she-wolves that needed to vent about their overbearing mates. That earned her a growl, which she took as a promise for fun things to come. Jacque had given up trying to reason with Decebel or Fane or any other male wolf. She'd come to the conclusion that their heads were just too thick for anything reasonable to penetrate through. It was amazing how much less frustration she felt when she wasn't trying to bang her head against the stubborn, unmoving will of a male Canis lupus.

"Wow Jac, tell us how you really feel," Jen snorted. "You went down the body bag road and all."

Jacque shrugged. "I'm pregnant. I get to use the 'I can be as blunt as I want' card because I also carry the membership card of 'I'm making a life, what's your excuse?'"

Jen held up her hand balled into a fist to her best friend. "I'm totally digging you prego. I think Fane should keep you on a continual baby making schedule. Pop one out and bam, put one back in that oven."

Jacque bumped Jen's fist as she laughed. "You are seriously disturbed, Jen."

"I could have been a tad more anatomically correct in my baby making description," Jen pointed out.

"True, you definitely showed restraint."

"So." Jen cleared her throat and Jacque could tell she was hesitant to say whatever it was that was on her mind, which was weird for her blonde friend. "How is your fur ball doing? Still reliving the hell of the In-Between at night?"

Ahh, Jacque thought, *that's why she was hesitant.* Only a select few in the pack knew that Fane was dealing with some intense issues. It was a touchy subject for a male wolf to admit he was struggling with anything. The only person Jacque had spoken to about it was Jen. Sally would have made that list as well, but she was MIA on whatever thing it was Peri deemed important enough to steal away the Serbia pack healer.

"He went to Vasile."

Jen's head snapped up and her piercing blue eyes met Jacque's. "He willingly sought out help from another male? Are you two still…,"

"Good grief, Jen, I'm not going down that road right now."

"I was going to say are you two still talking, you perv," Jen grumbled as she picked Thia up and grabbed a diaper from the diaper bag sitting by the couch.

Jacque watched her best friend as she changed Thia's diaper, and her own hand trailed to her swollen stomach. She absentmindedly rubbed circles on her stomach as she dreamed of what it would be like once her child was born.

Though she knew it was a little too late to worry about it then, she wondered if she was ready to be a mom. Could she be what her child would need? Or would she wind up screwing up royally? What if she and Fane didn't agree on how to raise him or her? What if—her thought was cut off by Jen's voice.

"Hey, earth to knocked-up chick," Jen said as she snapped her fingers in Jacque's face. She'd finished changing Thia's diaper and had placed the child back on her blanket on the floor. She was such an easy baby. Jacque had decided it wasn't fair that someone as contrary as Jen had ended up with such a pleasant child.

"What's going on in that red head of yours?"

Jacque laid her head back on the arm of the couch and let out a long sigh. "I'm just having pre-mother jitters I guess."

"You were raised by one of the best ladies I know. How can you be worried?" Jen asked as she raised Jacque's feet so she could sit at the end of the couch.

"Weren't you scared that you wouldn't be a good mom?" Jacque asked looking at her friend.

Jen shook her head. "I was too busy worrying about how to keep her alive once she was born and what my bull headed mate was up to."

Jacque nodded. "Oh, yeah, good point."

"Red, you're going to be a great mom. You won't be perfect, but hell, who is? We are bound to screw them up in some way.

The point is to just make sure it's something they can get counseling for later."

Jacque laughed. "Only you would give that kind of sage parenting advice."

"What kind of advice is my mate passing out this time," Decebel asked as he strode into the room. His eyes never left Jen, though he was addressing Jacque.

"Parenting advice," Jacque answered.

Decebel chuckled. "I will admit she's a very good mother to our pup. Though she does tend to use her to manipulate me."

Jen raised a brow at him. "I will use anything in my arsenal when it comes to the likes of you, B. We females have to be ready to stand up to you stubborn, pig-headed males. A little manipulation won't hurt you."

He reached down and picked up their daughter and she looked even smaller in his muscular arms. Decebel was a very good daddy. He adored Thia and Jacque thought it amazing to see such a stern man soften under the power of a little baby.

"Enough advice, woman." He reached out his other hand for Jen. "It's Thia's nap time."

A wide smile spread across her face. "I love nap time."

Jacque groaned. "I don't even want to know."

Jen took Dec's hand and let him pull her to her feet. As she gathered up their things, she looked over at Jacque and the gleam in her eyes was enough to let her know the next words out of her mouth would not be innocent.

"Don't judge, Red. Nap time is not just for Thia's wellbeing. You know how cranky I get if Decebel neglects his husbandly duties."

"I do not want to know anything about nap time or his husbandly duties."

Decebel tugged Jen's hand and nodded to Jacque. "We're headed back to the Serbia pack mansion. Tell Fane I'd like to speak with him when he's ready."

Jacque watched them leave, a slight frown settled on her face. She had a clue what Decebel wanted to talk with Fane about. She was just surprised that the Alpha was willing to. Decebel was a man of few words and not one to really share with anyone other than Jen. He must be very concerned about Fane to be willing to discuss the issues Fane was having.

She let out another sigh and closed her eyes, attempting to will away her worries. Jacque knew that worrying didn't fix anything. It would only cause her to lose sleep. Unfortunately, knowing something wasn't good for you and stopping, because of that knowledge, wasn't even in the same ballpark.

Once again she was at a loss as to how to help her mate. It wasn't as bad as the first time because at least now he was talking with her about it, but it frustrated her to no end to not be able to help him get past it.

Even more frustrating was that she was the cause of his pain and fear. The things that he had seen and heard in the In-Between all had to do with her. If she wasn't a part of his life, if she wasn't his mate, he wouldn't have had to endure things that were every male Canis lupus's nightmare. She was sure that Fane could have handled anything else. He would have been able to move past any painful situation, so long as it didn't concern her. It ate at her insides like a hungry parasite that she was his bane, his weakness, when all she wanted to be was a source of comfort and strength for him.

Jacque thought back to the actions Decebel had taken when he had realized what he needed to do to save Thia's life. Perhaps, it was time for Jacque to take her own desperate measures to help Fane. Maybe it was time to consider talking to the Great Luna and making a sacrifice for her true mate that would spare him all of the pain he was going through. It would probably destroy her, but it would mean that her mate was whole again. It would mean that he could move forward with his life. She would give up anything for him, even the life they'd built together if it meant he would be happy again.

Chapter 2

The crisp, late autumn air rippled through Fane's fur as he ran. The forest around their pack mansion had become a place of refuge for him. Though nothing could take the place of Jacquelyn's presence and comfort, the forest was a place for him to go when he wanted to give his mate a break from having to put up with his ever changing moods.

The trees surrounding him were tall, creating a fortress of enveloping protection. The bushes, limbs, and leaves were like fingers combing through his fur, welcoming him back as he ran through and around them. The dirt beneath his paws was cool and rich giving him good traction. He was made to be a part of the nature around him. His wolf craved the call of the wild, and Fane allowed him to answer it as often as he could. The only thing that would have made it better was having their mate running beside them.

She should be by our side always, his wolf growled at him. Fane understood the desire to have her with them all the time, but the man in him knew it simply wasn't feasible. His wolf grumbled at this but said no more on the matter.

"Decebel asked me to tell you that when you are ready he would like to speak to you." Jacque's voice invaded his mind and warmth flooded him as it always did when she used their bond.

"I'm out running now and close to their territory. I'll just go see him now." He paused before adding. *"Unless you need me."*

"I always need you, wolf-man, but I can spare you for a little while."

He chuckled at her playfulness. It was one of the things his wolf loved most about her. *"How is our child?"*

"At the moment, asleep. Which is a nice break from the kicks to the ribs I've been getting," she told him. He could feel her anxiety as she thought about their coming baby. They had talked a little about the fears that she had, but because of what Fane was dealing with, it hadn't been enough. He should be making sure that she was happy, healthy, and excited about their pup. But instead, he'd been a

lousy mate only able to focus on his own fears.

"I love you, Jacquelyn. I'll be home soon."

"Love you back, wolf-man."

He felt her pull away from him and was surprised when she shut her end of the bond down tight. Fane came to a sudden stop as his wolf briefly took control. His beast didn't like it when their mate shut down the bond. He struggled not to turn around and race back to her. He knew she was fine. Maybe she just needed an emotional break from all of his turmoil. The thought constricted his lungs making it difficult to breathe. Was he ever going to be the mate she needed him to be?

Fane regained control and forced his wolf to once again head toward the Serbia pack mansion. As he ran and the bond continued to stay closed, Fane vowed then that he would change things. Whatever he had to do in order to heal whatever it was that was broken inside of him, he would do it.

***

"What are you going to say to Fane?" Jen asked Decebel as she lay in their bed with her head resting against his warm chest as his hand stroked her back lazily. As she had planned, nap time for Thia had turned into mama and daddy time for them. Jen knew that Decebel had other things he needed to be doing, pack management things, but he always put her first. If she said she needed time with him, then he made it happen and for that she loved him even more than she had the day she married him.

He was quiet for a few minutes but she didn't ask again. She knew he would answer when he had decided how to word his response. Decebel was anything but hasty when it came to words, which of course was the complete opposite of Jen. Another thing she appreciated and loved about him, even if it did annoy the crap out of her when they were arguing.

"I'm going to make a suggestion," Decebel finally spoke. "One of the hardest things for us dominant males to do is ask for help. We feel as though we should be capable to handle anything and everything because that capability is what makes us dominant. In the wild, our cousins live and die by the survival of the fittest. Females pick their mates based on who the strongest male is. Pack Alphas are chosen by battles between wolves that are determined to show that they are the one dominant, strong enough and powerful enough to lead. Though we are more civilized than our cousins, we still feel those drives to a certain extent."

"Really?" Jen asked with wide eyes and then lifted a brow at him. "I never would have guessed that," she said dryly.

Decebel smacked her on the behind as he huffed. "Behave female."

Her lips quirked up in a small smile and she would have retorted, but she decided to let it go because of the worry she could see in his eyes. "What has you so worried, Dec?" she asked in a voice she only used with him or Thia. They were the only two who brought out the gentler side that hid beneath the shield she kept in place for the rest of the world.

"Fane is still so very young. He's mated and been through much that has caused him to have to mature quickly, but he hasn't yet reached that place of confidence that comes with age." His fingers began brushing through her blonde locks as she lay her head back on his chest and waited for him to continue. "There are some experiences that can break a person, Jennifer. There are some things that happen to a person that they just can't come back from."

The ominous sound in his voice had her pushing up on her forearms to look at him. "You think that's what's happened to Fane?" She knew that her question held serious doubt because she couldn't believe that Fane could ever be broken; just like the idea of Decebel ever being broken was laughable to her. They were male Canis lupus—strong, powerful, dominant, Alpha—and they kicked butts while taking names. How could any of them possibly be broken?

Decebel held her gaze as he answered her. "I don't know. After the fight he and Costin had, he seemed to get better and I thought he had finally made it through the darkness to the other side, but something has pulled him back in."

Jen was about to say something in response but there was a knock at their door that had her snapping her mouth closed.

"Speak," Decebel growled. Jen grinned. He hated having his time with her interrupted.

"Fane Lupei is here to see you, Alpha," the wolf on the other side of their door answered.

"Well, that didn't take long," Jen mumbled as her mate climbed out of their bed, giving her one of her favorite shows—the Decebel getting dressed show. She liked the Decebel getting *undressed* show better, but she'd take what she could get.

He glanced at her as he pulled on his pants. "You have no shame, woman."

A wicked grin spread across her face as she propped her chin up on her hand. "And you hate that you love that about me."

He chuckled and slipped on a shirt. "As long as your lack of shame only extends to me, I'm more than happy to endure it. It's when you decide to share that particular quality with others that I am annoyed."

"Annoyed? Seriously, what are you the king of understatement-ville? Annoyed is not even close to what you become."

He shrugged, something he'd picked up from her. "I say annoyed; you say ready to rip someone apart limb from limb."

She shook her head at him and shooed him away. "Go do what you gotta do, Alpha. I'll be patiently awaiting your return."

He gave her a crooked smile as he opened their door. "Baby, you don't do anything patiently."

Jen rolled her eyes and threw a pillow at the closing door. "I put up with you, you butthead. That's the ultimate act of patience," she called out and despite the shut door she knew he had heard her.

"I swear if he wasn't so yummy I'd push him out a window," she grumbled to the empty room.

Chapter 3

Jacque knew that Fane was going to be upset with her because she'd closed her end of the bond, but it was necessary. If Fane knew what she was about to do, he would be beyond livid—not that she would blame him.

Jacque slipped the book she'd been reading back onto the shelf in the library. She had to do some research before she could put her plan into action. Thankfully, she'd become very familiar with pack history after doing so much research searching for information about the dark forest. She'd reviewed many of the ancient books in the pack archives that had been long forgotten. One of those books just happened to be about the Fates.

She grabbed a jacket and her small bag packed with supplies and headed for the back door hoping that she wouldn't run into Vasile or Alina. Jacque hadn't realized she'd been holding her breath until she was outside in the cool air. Fall was quickly turning into winter and it wouldn't be long until the mountains around them would be blanketed in glistening snow. A shiver crawled down her spine as she remembered the times in the past year that they had to trek through the snow. There had been so much that she'd done since meeting Fane—things that she would never have done had she not been his mate.

Her heart took a nose dive for her toes as she thought about all that she would be giving up if she was allowed to follow through with her plan. Jacque shook her head, unwilling to dwell on the negative. She was doing this for Fane, regardless of what it meant for her.

She moved as quickly and as quietly as she could with her six month protruding belly. Jacque was glad Jen was not with her because she would no doubt be giving her a play-by-play commentary on how hilarious Jacque's pregnant butt looked tromping through the forest. Then again, Jen would be ripping her a new one for even considering what she had in mind, not that Jen could talk. With all the half cocked, hair brained ideas she'd come up with over the years, she really shouldn't be able to judge Jacque. When the frustration of an argument that hadn't happened began to bubble up inside of her, Jacque realized what she was doing. "Holy crap, I've resorted to imaginary fighting with Jen in order to justify my actions," she muttered as she stepped over a fallen tree. She felt her baby kick her as though agreeing with her ridiculousness. Okay, so maybe she had fallen off the deep end, it wouldn't be the first time.

As the climb began to steepen, she crested a hill and looked around her. The air felt as if it was being sucked from her lungs against her will. Jacque's head turned slowly as she took in the forest around her. It was not the familiar forest that surrounded her Romanian pack mansion. The forest where she currently found herself was miles away. She turned to the right and saw the pond that she had walked into while under the trance Desdemona had placed on her. The same pond in which Fane had dove into in an attempt to save her. How had she gotten that far from the mansion in a matter of minutes? Peri had told them many times during their journeys into the forest that the forest had eyes and ears. Even though this was the human realm, there was still a certain amount of magic present because of all the supernatural beings that chose to dwell here. It shouldn't have surprised her that the forest had influenced her trek, but that didn't mean it wasn't disconcerting.

In all honesty, she had no idea where she was going. The book she'd been reading in the pack library had given specific details on how to contact the Fates, but not a precise location. The paragraph in question had read:

There is a way to contact the Fates, but you do so at your own peril. The Fates are not to be trifled with and do not like being summoned by mortals. But they occasionally choose to answer if they feel the reason for contact is one that is worthy of their attention. If you do decide to pursue them, then these are the things you must know. First, you must be far from civilization. The Fates typically choose to cross over from their own realm into areas of our realm that are unspoiled by humans and their industrialization. It is best to attempt to contact them near dusk when the sun is departing to make way for its sister to take up residence in her place in the sky. As with most requests made to supernatural beings, an offering is required. A blood offering is the most respected but be careful where you let your blood fall. There are beings that will be attracted to the power the Fates radiate and might come seeking out

the source. You do not want your blood to fall into
the care of any who could use it against you. Once
you have picked a destination, you will make your
offering and then speak the following words:

I have come to request an audience with those
who know past, present, and future.
Humbly I ask to present my request to you.
I give an offering, a sacrifice of blood.
And I kneel awaiting your answer.

Jacque didn't particularly look forward
to the whole sacrificing her blood part, but
she would do what was necessary. After
another half hour of walking, she came to an
area where several large boulders protruded
from the mountainside. Several of them
looked perfect to use as a table to set out the
bowl, towel, and knife she'd brought to
perform the ritual. She set down her bag and
stretched her tired muscles, tilting her head
back and gazing up at the tree tops that
towered above her. She'd spent most of the
day doing research, which had eaten up a lot
of her daylight, but she'd still made it in time
to begin at dusk. The sun was already
commencing its slow decent and less light
was filtering through the branches to the

forest floor. The forest was still and an eerie silence surrounded her. Jacque rubbed her arms absently as the hair seemed to stand on end.

She shook off the creepy sensation and turned back to her backpack and began unpacking the things she'd need. The book hadn't said to bring a candle, but it hadn't said not to either. The woods would grow dark quickly and, though she had her wolf to assist with seeing in the dark, the human part of her felt safer with some sort of light to break through the darkness.

Once everything was laid out on the improvised table, Jacque took several deep breaths and shook out her hands, attempting to rid herself of the jitters that had suddenly began to infect her limbs. She knew the minute that Fane had felt her nerves because she felt his push against the closed bond. Picturing a solid brick wall in her mind, she fortified the barricade between them. It sickened her wolf to cause such separation between them and their mate, but she couldn't risk him breaking through. Part of her wanted to ask for his forgiveness, but if everything worked out, he wouldn't even remember her so the request would be futile.

With one final glance up at the sky beyond the trees, she confirmed that it was time to begin. Jacque lit the candle. She'd even remembered a lighter, which was impressive given her forgetful pregnant mindset lately, and then she picked up the knife.

As she pressed the blade to the palm of her hand and held it over the bowl to catch the falling flow of blood, the words she'd memorized flew from her lips, filling up the silence that had suddenly descended around her. Jacque felt as if all of nature was holding its breath—watching, waiting, and wondering—just as she was to see if the Fates would make an appearance. And if they did, would they grant her request? Once the words were spoken and her blood coated the bottom of the bowl, she wrapped the towel tightly around her palm. From the kneeling position Jacque had taken during the invocation, she bowed her head and waited to see if her world would be changed forever.

Chapter 4

Fane was attempting to focus on Decebel's words but his wolf kept pulling his attention back to their mate. Sweat broke out across his forehead as feelings of sorrow, fear, and apprehension swept through him. He also felt a rush of adrenaline that had his hands twitching just a little, which meant it wasn't his own adrenaline he was feeling—it was Jacquelyn's. Fane reached for her again by mentally pushing against the wall between them, and—to his utter shock—he felt his mate making it stronger, putting all of her will into keeping him from getting through.

Something is wrong, his wolf growled to him.

"What was your first clue?" Fane snapped, not realizing he'd spoken out loud until Decebel questioned him. Fane looked up, his unfocused eyes clearing and seeing the Alpha's concerned gaze roving over his face.

"Are you alright?" Decebel asked.

Fane nearly choked on a laugh. Was he alright? No, he wasn't. He was as far from alright in that moment as he had been since the first time he'd let the memories break him. But now he knew it was not simply his own problems that were troubling him.

"Something is wrong with Jacquelyn," he growled, unable to hide his frustration.

"Is she hurt? Is the baby okay?" The Alpha took a step toward him, his natural instinct to protect kicking in full force.

"She's blocking me. I can't feel her; I only know she is alive."

Decebel's frown grew even darker. "If she's blocking you, then she's up to something. Our mates are notorious for digging themselves into graves while making sure we remain ignorant to their exploits."

Fane's gut told him that Decebel was right. Whatever was causing the strong emotions in his mate, it was of her own making. That didn't, in any way, reassure him that she was safe and okay.

"Why do the two of you look like you've sucked on a pound of lemon wedges?" Jen asked as she sauntered into the room with Thia on her hip. "Seriously dudes, the '*I might have a grape in my butt I'm squeezing*' look just does nothing for you two no matter how hot you are."

"Jacque is blocking Fane from her mind," Decebel answered, sounding every bit as irritated as Fane felt. He didn't bother to respond to her snark.

"Oh dear," Jen crooned. "What is my redheaded girl up to, I wonder?"

"Jennifer, if you know something it wouldn't be smart to keep it from her mate."

Jen eyed her mate and Fane knew it was a look that behooved Dec to shut his mouth. Fane had been on the receiving end of that look many times from his own mate. Too bad male werewolves were too hardheaded to learn.

Decebel blew a sharp breath as he pinched the bridge of his nose. "You know how protective we are of our females."

"You say protective; I say bordering on unhealthy psychopathic codependency syndrome. But let's not get technical or anything," Jen bit out through clinched teeth.

To Fane and Jen's surprise, Decebel didn't take the bait. "Do you know anything?" he asked simply.

Jen stared at him for several seconds before responding. "You know it's not any fun when you don't react."

"Perhaps, I've finally learned my lesson," her mate countered.

Jen snorted. "You, a male Canis lupus, learning his lesson? That's like saying it's possible for penguins to tap dance out of your ass every time you fart."

Had Fane not been so concerned about his mate, he would have given that point to Jen. He was sure one day her witty comebacks would make their way into a book for all of humanity to experience.

With Decebel left glaring at her, she turned to Fane. "She didn't tell me anything. I asked her how you were doing, tried to give her some much needed bedroom advice, and talked about girl crap you guys aren't privy to know about. That's all. I didn't get the 'I'm up to something' vibe from her at all." Jen paused and tapped her lip. Thia was attempting to grab her finger, no doubt so she could shove it into her little mouth and gnaw on it. "That is a little disconcerting. Somebody look out the window and tell me if the sky is falling because that's as likely as Red being able to keep something from me."

"Maybe she wasn't up to anything. Maybe she decided to do something after she left you," Fane suggested, sounding calmer than he felt.

Jen shook her head. "I still should have sensed something. I've known her since she squeezed herself out of her mom's girly bits." She walked over to one of the loveseats in Decebel's office and sat down putting Thia in her lap. The worry that was marring her mate's and Fanes' faces was now mirrored on her own.

Fane turned toward the door intending to leave and go sniff out his mate, literally, but Jen's voice stopped him.

"Maybe I should go," she said and stood and handed Thia to Decebel. "Sometimes a girl needs a little space. And if that's what she's doing, putting a little space between you two, then you tracking her down might not go over real well."

Fane's wolf was practically roaring at him to ignore the female and go after their mate. To his beast there was no such thing as space between them. And though Fane knew that Jen's words could be true, he didn't like to think that his mate needed space from him.

She is ours, no one else's, his wolf snarled. But Fane knew that wasn't true. Yes, Jacque was their mate, but she was also Jen's best friend, Vasile and Alina's daughter-in-law, and pack member to the Romanian pack. There were many who would claim a piece of her, and he knew that wasn't a bad thing, but his wolf didn't like to share—nor did Fane—but the man in him had learned to be more reasonable. *She is ours to protect,* Fane told him, *but we are not all she needs and, perhaps, now Jen is right.* He felt his wolf trying to take over, unwilling to accept the man's decision, but Fane was able to maintain control.

"You will let Decebel know she is safe so he can tell me." He had meant it to come out as a question but Fane knew that is not how it had sounded.

Jen quirked a brow up at him. "Because I know how hard it is for you males to relinquish control to another, I will ignore the fact that you just gave me an order." She turned to her mate and rose up on her toes to press a quick kiss to his lips and then left without waiting for Decebel to agree to her actions.

"She has taken well to being an Alpha female," Fane said as he took a seat and prepared to wait—something he was not good at—for news about his mate.

Decebel sat across from him with Thia cradled in his large arms. His amber eyes met Fane's, revealing the tight control the Alpha himself struggled to maintain. Fane looked away out of respect for him.

"She has," Decebel agreed though his voice was tight. "She is the mother of my child, light to my darkness, and other half of my soul, but that doesn't change the fact that she is also a pain in my—" He paused looking down at his daughter. Decebel rarely cursed and especially not in front of Thia, regardless of the fact that she couldn't yet understand him. "Well, you get my point." He sighed, leaning back on the couch that his large form dwarfed.

Fane understood to an extent what he was saying. Jacque wasn't as bold and outspoken as Jen, but then few were. But his redheaded mate had a temper, and she definitely didn't let him dictate to her, which most of the time was more of a turn-on than an annoyance. No male of his species wanted their female to be compliant all of the time; just as none of their females wanted a male that would cower from her outbursts or lay down stupidly while she ran off into danger. The friction that existed between them was, ironically, tied directly to the passion they felt for each other. So even though he was sitting there worrying about her, frustrated with her actions and ready to tear through the forest to go after her, he wouldn't change a thing about her.

"Yes," Fane finally spoke. "I definitely get your point. I've asked you before, 'Would you have it any other way?' Now I ask you again after the time you've been mated and the things you've been through together. Would you have it any other way, Alpha?"

A sly smile took the place of his scowl. "And be bored out of my mind with a female that catered to my every whim? No way. I'll take worry, fighting, fear, frustration, and all the other emotions that come with being mated to a feisty female over boredom any day."

They both sat in contemplative silence, though Fane was barely holding himself still. It felt so unnatural not to be the one checking on his mate and the one fixing whatever it was that she needed fixed.

"Since we're here and we've got nothing but time," Decebel said breaking the quiet, "why don't you tell me what it is that has you thinking you are incapable?"

Fane's eyes snapped up. "Why is that the conclusion you've come to regarding my battles?"

"Because I was young once upon a time. I remember what it was like to have the confidence that is innate in a dominate wolf and to then have it ripped from your grasp because of something that was out of your control."

Fane knew the Alpha was speaking about his sister's death.

"I did not handle what happened to Cosmina with great poise," he continued. "I broke under the weight of the guilt I felt for being unable to save her." Decebel narrowed his eyes on him, not in a stern manner but a calculating one. "What each of us endured in the In-Between left us wounded in some way. Some of those wounds run deeper than others. Instead of just grazing the skin, the wound has pierced muscle, tendons, and, in some cases, even broken bones. A shallow wound will not heal at the same rate as a deeper wound, and sometimes when a wound has begun to heal it endures more trauma and is reopened. Something has reopened your wound that was just beginning to scar, and the scar had not had the time to harden."

Fane closed his eyes, remembering the peace he had felt when he finally let it go. Why had he picked it back up again? He kept coming back to the same questions. What had caused him to begin having the dreams again, which in turn renewed the flames of the memories he thought he'd doused?

"I have this timeline mapped out in my mind, and I keep going over it and over it trying to figure out at what point I picked up the burden that I thought I'd let go of," Fane told him as he leaned forward with his elbows resting on his knees and his hands laced together clenching and unclenching.

"Have you come to any conclusion?"

Fane shook his head. "There hasn't been anything, no so-called trauma, that has happened since getting the females back. Things have been so calm."

Decebel glanced down at his sleeping daughter as he responded. "Does the trauma always have to come from a negative source?"

Fane wanted to growl at he continued metaphors but bit it back because he knew

Decebel was just trying to help him. "What do you mean?"

"Sometimes wounds are reopened during a time of celebration or fun. I've had many battle wounds open up while sparring with other wolves, and the sparring was all in good nature with no animosity between us, and yet that something good was still traumatic to the wound."

"Are you deliberately dragging this out in order to distract me?"

Decebel chuckled. "Okay, perhaps, my age is showing through my council. What I'm trying to say is you have recently had something that is worthy of great celebration happen to you. But regardless of how good it is, it is also going to change your life in a very big way. Maybe you should consider the upcoming birth of your first child as the possible trauma to your wound."

"I'm not unhappy about Jacquelyn being pregnant," Fane said as he shot to his feet and began to pace. "I know that we are both young and didn't really plan for this to happen so soon, but neither of us regrets it."

"I'm not implying that you do," Decebel parried. "I'm simply saying that maybe the stress, because there is stress when having a baby whether you are happy about it or not, has caused some of those worries and doubts to resurface."

Fane continued to pace back and forth across the room. His mind was replaying Decebel's words over and over again as he considered the truth that was in the Alpha's suggestion. It was true that Fane was over the moon about their baby, but it was also true that he and Jacquelyn both had worries over being young parents. They would be foolish to think that they knew exactly what they were in for. Fane considered the things that he had thought about in regards to being a father, things he had pushed back because of the other worries rearing their ugly heads once again. He made a sharp turn heading back in the opposite direction and then his feet froze as the truth came crashing down on him like a bucket of ice water.

His head slowly turned to look down at Decebel. "I understand," he breathed out. The weight was still there, but he finally understood what the weight was from. "Before, when I couldn't get past it, it was because at first I couldn't let go of the things I'd seen. And once I moved on from that, it was because I felt as though I had failed my mate."

Decebel nodded his understanding but said nothing.

"And after I finally accepted that what had happened was beyond my control, I was able to let go of the burden. But now there is another who will fall under the cloak of my protection. Someone small, vulnerable, and completely dependent on me and Jacquelyn." His voice shook as he bowed his head in surrender. "And it scares me to death."

Chapter 5

Jen walked briskly out of the mansion. A quick retreat was always best when attempting to pull the wool over a wolf's eyes. Jen was a little surprised that Fane had bought the BS she'd been spewing about Jacque needing space. Granted, there were definitely times when a girl needed some breathing room from the overbearing men they were mated to. But, in this instance, Jen knew that was not what was going on with her friend. Jacque was in too much turmoil over what Fane was dealing with to want space from him. If anything, she probably wanted to be by his side, curled up in the safety of his embrace, just to have the reassurance that—despite his ghosts—he was still willing to let her in. For Jacque to have closed the bond after having Fane do that very thing only a few months ago, instead of letting his mate be what he needed, meant she was in some sort of deep defecation. Okay, so that was a ridiculous way to put it, but she *was* trying to curb her foul tongue to be a better example for Thia. "Oh, the things we do for our little drool factories," she muttered as she climbed into the black SUV that she repeatedly told her mate was ridiculously cliché' for werewolves to drive. He didn't really care what she thought was ridiculous—his words. She couldn't repeat what she'd said back since she was trying to tame her tongue.

As she headed in the direction of the Romanian pack mansion, Jen kept expecting Dec to contact her through their bond. To her surprise, she pulled up into the driveway without so much as a 'get your cute butt home'. It might have been smart of her to consider why her mate was acting out of character, but she didn't want to take the time. She knew it wouldn't be long before Fane came to the same conclusion she had about Jacque shutting the bond, and then he would be a pissed off Canis lupus who'd been duped by his mate's friend—and it was not for the first time.

As soon as she started up the front steps to the Romanian pack mansion, Jen let her wolf's senses take over and picked up Jacque's scent. Only it wasn't headed into the building. Jen turned and looked out at the forest that had caused her one too many headaches.

"What are you up to, little Red?" she muttered under her breath as she followed Jacque's trail into the forest. Jen realized, after twenty minutes of walking, that she clearly hadn't thought her plan through. "A coat would have been smart," she huffed at herself, "and earmuffs, gloves, a canteen of hot chocolate. Bloody hell, Jennifer, you act like you've never trekked through the cold mountains before." She couldn't help laughing at her ironic statement considering in recent months the forest and mountains had practically been home. Now, as she once again trudged through the foliage, she wondered what could have caused her best friend to return to the woods that was home to many unseen supernatural beings.

Night was falling rapidly and the temperature was dropping as she climbed higher into the mountains. She'd considered phasing to her wolf, but she didn't like the vulnerability of being naked out here, even if it was only briefly while she put her clothes back on. Not to mention, she'd have to carry her clothes in her mouth.

"How is Jacque?" Her mate's voice flowed into her mind. She was surprised at how long he'd gone without reaching out to her, though he would have known in a heartbeat if something was wrong. Jen considered his question. She had to play her cards carefully or he and Fane would be ripping through the forest like obsessed mad men.

"She's good." Jen didn't specify that the 'she's' part was meant to be short for 'she *was*' and not 'she *is*'. So she wasn't technically lying. The last time she'd seen Jacque she *was* good.

"Has she explained why she is closing the bond between her and her mate?"

"Not in so many words," she hedged.

"What has she said?"

Jen could tell he was growing impatient with her, not that it was anything new. *"We haven't really made it to that part of the girl time. We've just been taking a stroll down memory lane. Again, not a lie,"* she thought to herself. They both had indeed strolled through the forest where tons of memories remained. They just hadn't been together while doing it.

"Do you think you could please ask her to let Fane know she's alright?" Even in her head she could hear the bite in his question.

"I can ask her. That doesn't mean that she will do it." Jen stopped to look around because she hadn't been paying attention in the least to where she was while she'd been answering Decebel's questions. She shivered when she saw her surroundings and realized where she was. The large boulders protruding from the mountain and deep crevices brought back not so happy memories. "Good times," she muttered as she remembered being pushed into one of those crevices by Martha, the she-wolf who'd fallen in love with a human and only wanted to be with him. Don't ask Jen why the nut job thought pushing her into the side of a mountain would make her dreams come true. Apparently, when crazy people do crazy crap it totally makes sense to them.

"Why is your heart beating so fast?" Decebel's question had her returning to the present, pushing back the memories of Martha and her craziness. Sometimes she appreciated how in tune her mate was to her. And other times she really wished he was as clueless as most women thought the male gender to be.

"Because I'm walking, briskly."

"You and Jacque?"

"Exactly, I am walking, and Jacque is walking, and it's at a speed that causes the heart to beat more quickly. This way blood can get oxygen to my muscles so that I can walk briskly." The words were just pouring out of her even as she screamed at herself to shut the hell up. She still hadn't lied, or at least she hoped not. It was probably a pretty good bet that Jacque really was, in that moment, walking. Crap, she was in a damn forest. What else do people do in a forest but walk? *Okay, so maybe there other things they could do,* she conceded with a sly grin.

"Other things, who, could do where?"

"Bloody hell does the man miss anything!" *"Listen, B, you know I love our little chats, especially when they get spicy, but I can't focus on you and Jacque at the same time. So I'm going to need you to skedaddle, while we continue our girl time."*

There was a long pause but she knew he hadn't retreated. It took everything in her not to beat her head against a tree when he finally spoke.

"So you're telling me that you and Jacque are having girl time while walking, briskly. Which has caused your heart beat to increase to get oxygen rich blood to your muscles so that you can walk, briskly.

And because it takes so much focus to walk briskly and talk about girl stuff, you need me to skedaddle?"

The undisguised humor laced with suspicion had Jen vowing that as soon as she saw him, she was going to kick him. The location of that kick was still up for debate.

"Exactly. So glad we're on the same page, K. Kiss Thia for me. Don't forget to sing to her, Don't wait up, love you, bye bye." Jen slammed the door on their bond. She was actually breathing hard as if she'd said all of that out loud and not just in her mind. She could feel Dec's frustration with her. She hadn't shut the bond completely, just enough that he couldn't read her every thought. Regardless, she knew she was going to get a lecture from her fur ball when she returned home. "This had better be worth it, Jacquelyn Lupei," she muttered as she continued through the now dark forest.

Using her wolf's sight, she had no trouble navigating around trees and bushes. And with her wolf's sense of smell, she had no problem knowing if there were bigger and badder predators near her. When she took a deep breath, attempting to check for that very thing, she suddenly realized that she could no longer detect Jacque's scent.

Jen turned in a slow circle, breathing in and out of her nose, attempting to regain her friend's trail. But all she smelled were the things that belonged in the forest. She stopped suddenly and tilted her head back a little further. *Except* that *smell,* she thought, *it doesn't belong.*

"Peace to you this night, Jennifer, mate to Decebel, Alpha female of the Serbia pack, beloved mother and friend."

Jen felt the sudden desire to have a three-year-old moment bubble up inside of her, and she had to force her feet to remain still instead of stomping. She had to bite her tongue so that she wouldn't allow herself to "word vomit" into the quiet, serene forest. One might ask why she suddenly felt the urge to act in such a way, and Jen would answer because every time this particular voice had popped up it meant crap was going to hit the fan. Jen was seriously tired of cleaning fans.

"Good evening, Great Luna," Jen said calmly as she turned to face the creator of her mate's race.

The Great Luna smiled serenely at her and Jen could see the understanding in her eyes. "I can understand why you might be leery of my appearance."

"It's just that we finally have a break, and I don't really feel like fighting a bunch of crazy ass—" Jen said then paused and corrected herself, "crazy butt—man, that just doesn't have the same kick behind it—supernatural bad guys right now." She shook her hands in front of her as though she was shaking off water. "Sorry, I digress. I just had a baby. Okay, so it was like six months ago, but seriously do you see what those things do to a girl's body? It takes time to bounce back, literally and figuratively, and frankly my bounce has not fully returned." Jen let out a quick huff, her brief tirade complete, and stared back at the deity.

"You have fought hard, on the battlefield and off. I do not come to you tonight to bring a fight to your door. It is your sister Jacquelyn that must battle, but hers is a different sort of war. She has a lesson to learn."

"Damn, I hate it when that happens," Jen muttered under her breath.

The Great Luna continued as though the she-wolf had said nothing. "It is not one that her mate can help her with, and yet

Decebel and Fane are already in search of you both. All I ask of you this night is to do what seems to come naturally to you." She paused and to Jen's surprise a slight smile curved her flawless lips. "A little distraction is in order."

Jen tried to keep her jaw from dropping open. The Great Luna had just asked her to keep Fane from his mate.

"Wait, wait." Jen shuffled her feet and put her hands on her hips. "You mean to tell me B and Fane are already on their way, and you want me to have a distraction ready? Do you know how long it takes to prepare something? I mean, I don't have a table. There's no music. Really, what do I have to work with? I got trees and dirt." Jen was now looking at her surroundings. She heard the Great Luna say something about having faith that she would figure it out, but Jen simply waved her off as she tapped a slender finger to her lips. "Distraction, distraction," she mumbled to herself as the wheels of her mind cranked to life. "Can't really do the whole lifting the shirt thing. Dec has so been there and done that. Can't do a pretend strip tease. Don't have any cards to play poker with." She continued tapping her finger against her lips as she thought of her options.

A plan began to form in her mind. "It won't be my best work," she huffed as she dropped to the ground and began rolling around getting herself dirty. She grabbed handfuls of dirt, spit on it, and then rubbed it all over her face. Next she reached up and tugged on her long pony tail causing it to loosen into a crooked mess. Jen looked down at her shirt and, despite the dirt, decided it was still too neat looking. She grabbed the bottom and jerked, causing a tear to rip across the bottom. She did this several more times, turning her shirt this way and that to spread the rips. Then she yanked off one of her shoes and threw it as hard as she could with her wolf's help, which was pretty dang far, into the woods.

"Okay, phase one, of Distract the Werewolves because the Great Luna Said So, is complete." She narrowed her eyes and pursed her lips. "DWWBGLSS." She shook her head. "That's going to need some work."

Jen tilted her head and attempted to listen. The forest was quiet. She couldn't hear the usual scuttle of nighttime critters. She knew how quiet wolves could be when they hunted, but she was pretty sure Decebel and Fane hadn't found her yet.

"Dec?" She pushed open the bond just a little as she reached out to him. She waited several heartbeats before speaking to him again. *"Decebel?"* It would probably serve her right for him to ignore her, but that didn't mean it wouldn't piss her off.

"What are you getting all worked up about, baby?" His voice came through low and sultry, sending shivers down her back. How dare he try to flirt with her when she was trying to figure out what he was up to and how dare he be up to something when mischief was supposed to be her specialty?

"I'm not worked up about anything. What would give you that idea?" Jen made sure to keep her thoughts about Jacque, the Great Luna, and her little distraction shut tightly away from her mate.

"You just sounded a little frantic."

"I did not sound frantic. So," she drew out the word before asking, *"What are you boys up to? Have you helped Fane deal with his demons and what not?"*

"We talked."

"And it went well?"

"It did."

Bloody hell, Jen thought, trying to get information from him is like trying to squeeze peanut oil from a damn lime. *"So what are you up to now?"* she asked trying to sound as casual as she could.

"Well, funny you should ask."

Jen felt the hackles on her neck rising—nota good sign.

"After we talked, Fane started thinking about Jacque and her strange behavior."

"She's a chick, B, and she's knocked up. It's really her prerogative to act strange."

"Yeah, but one thing that he said didn't make sense," Decebel continued as though she hadn't said a word. *"Jacque was so upset about him shutting her out when he was struggling before. He told me that for some reason it just didn't make sense that she would suddenly want space from him when she was so angry at him and hurt when he put space between them. So I helpfully suggested that maybe my mate, beautiful though she may be, didn't really know what the hell she was talking about. So I made the suggestion that, perhaps, we should come find you two."*

Jen's hands were on her hips and her foot was tapping out a steady beat as she glared at nothing because her mate wasn't standing in front of her to be glared at. *"So you're on your way here now?"*

"Yes."

Great. She threw her hands up in the air and tilted her head back. How was she supposed to make it look like she and Jacque had been attacked if she was calmly talking to him now?

"Are you guys at the mansion?" he asked her.

She grinned as a light bulb moment happened. She didn't answer right away.

"Jennifer?"

She wanted to feel bad about the worry she heard in his voice, but then she remembered him saying that she didn't know what the hell she was talking about, and all her sympathy flew out the window.

"Jennifer answer me!"

Time to put her famous acting skills into action. Okay, so maybe they weren't famous but they should have been. *"OH CRAP!"* she yelled through their bond. *"RUN, JACQUE!"*

"JENNIFER! What is going on? Where are you?" Decebel's growl and command called to her wolf. The stupid hussy thought he was attractive when he went all Alpha on them.

"I told you we were walking, briskly, because we needed some air. Clean air is good for a pregnant chick you know. So here we are out walking in the woods."

"You went into the woods at NIGHT, BY YOURSELVES!" he snarled and she could feel his sudden urgency.

Jen momentarily forgot her roll. *"Um, we're werewolves too, remember? It's not like we're helpless."*

"Then what is going on? Why are you yelling at Jacque to run?"

"Crap!" Jen snapped out as she realized she'd let herself get distracted. *"We might have run into a little problem while walking. Look, I can't think and talk to you at the same time. You and Fane just get your fine butts into the mountains behind the mansion. I don't know how far we've gone but Jacque just took off and . . ."* She paused for effect before yelling. *"DAMN! There went my shoe! Hurry up, B. I really had no desire to be chased by wild pigs yet again—or like, ever."*

"Pigs? Jennifer what are you talking—"

She cut him off not wanting to keep talking. *"JUST HURRY! I have to find Jacque."* And once again she tightened her side of the bond down.

Jen closed her eyes tightly and rubbed her temple with her fingers. "Ok, Great Luna," she said into the quiet night. "I know you're listening. I just told my mate we were being chased by pigs. Now, since this was your idea I'm asking for a little help. He isn't going to believe a thing I say if he gets here and nothing smells like pigs. So I'm going to start jogging that way." She pointed in front of her which was away from the mansion. "And I need some help with making his other senses believe what my appearance and freaking out are going to be conveying. Deal?"

Jen didn't wait to see if the deity responded. She started off at a brisk job, zigzagging through the trees. After a quarter of a mile she paused and looked behind her.

A huge grin spread across her face and she couldn't help the small chuckle of laughter. "I think that should do it. Thank you for that," she told the Great Luna who had indeed heard her request and fulfilled it rather nicely. The ground Jen had passed over now looked as though not only her feet had trampled across it but as though a pack of wild bores had run through it crashing and clomping along tearing up the land and foliage around them. Even when Jen took a breath in, she caught the scent of the wild boars as if they had indeed been there.

She turned back and started off at her brisk jog again. She knew it wouldn't be much longer and her mate and Fane would catch up to her. Then the real acting would begin.

Chapter 6

"**O**pen your eyes, Jacquelyn," a soothing voice, one that most definitely didn't belong to the Fates, said from behind where she knelt. She blinked several times to clear her vision and looked up into the night sky. Stars, more numerous than she could count, stared back at her.

Jacque stood slowly and turned to face the Great Luna. When her eyes met those of the goddess, Jacque felt as though she'd been caught with her hand in the cookie jar. The cold mountain wind felt even sharper on her skin as she felt her face heat up with the guilt that had been building inside of her.

"It never ceases to amaze me how selfless my children can be."

Jacque felt as if there was a very distinct *but* that was headed her way.

The Great Luna began walking slowly, her steps measured and smooth, in a circle around the area Jacque had claimed as her destination for the ritual. Her hands where clasped together in front of her and her posture was relaxed, though her shoulders didn't slump and her back was perfectly erect.

"Before you decided what was best for your mate, did you stop to consider what the effect of your actions might be?" There was no accusation in her voice, no condemnation. It was simply a question.

Jacque hated to admit that she hadn't considered anything except how it would benefit Fane. She hadn't considered any other factor, because she feared that if she thought too much about the decision, then she might not be able to go through with it. Her silence was answer enough.

"If you will permit me," the goddess continued, "before you proceed any further, I would like to take you on a journey. I will warn you now that it will not be an easy one, but then," she said and turned to meet Jacque's eyes, "we both know you are no stranger to challenges."

"Do I have a choice?" Jacque asked.

"Of course. You always have a choice. I will not force your will."

Jacque didn't know why she'd asked. She knew that she would go with the Great Luna because she genuinely believed the goddess had her best interest at heart. "Well," she heaved a tired sigh, "might as well face the firing squad."

The Great Luna reached out her hand and Jacque took it without hesitation. There was a sudden gust of wind and then a pulling sensation that took Jacque's breath away. It lasted only a moment and then, abruptly, it was over and all was still around them once again. But they were no longer in the forest.

Jacque's eyes widened as she realized she was standing in the living room of her house back in Texas. She watched as her mom walked out of the kitchen, and Jacque had to hold herself back from running to her and flinging herself into her mother's arms. She hadn't realized how much she'd missed her mother over the months or how badly she needed to be held and told that everything would be alright. She realized that it didn't matter how old a person grew or how their life changed, there was just something about a mom that no one could replace.

"She cannot see or hear you," the Great Luna warned before Jacque could attempt to say anything to Lilly.

"Is this like the Canis lupus version of the whole Christmas Carol thing?" Jacque asked as she watched herself walk into the living room. "Holy blowholes, are my hips really that big?" she muttered, momentarily distracted.

"This is what could have been," the goddess answered. "If you and Fane had failed to meet, to complete the unique bond that you had with *only* one another, then these are the events that would have come to pass."

Jacque didn't like the sound of that because she was pretty sure it meant that she was going to be seeing more than just her own could-have-beens. "So what day is it? Should I have met Fane already?"

"This is several days after you would have met Fane. But in this reality, he did not come to Cold Spring as an exchange student. And since Fane was not here to stop him, another has stepped in ready to make a claim on you."

There was a knock at the door and her mother walked over and answered it. Jacque's eyes widened as she watched her mother speak cordially with none other than Lucas Steele.

"He's dead," she whispered and instinctively took a step back. To her shock she watched herself walk over to the door and smile—bloody hell, she actually smiled at the jerk! "What am I doing? Don't smile at him, you shameless hussy," Jacque growled at her past self.

"Trent still broke off your relationship because he was still threatened by Lucas to stay away from you. You met Lucas at a gas station. You were having trouble with the pump and he saw you and came over to help you."

"How kind of him," Jacque huffed as her eyes narrowed on Lucas and herself chatting like old friends. Jacque feels a warm hand on her arm and then the pulling sensation is back. In a matter of seconds they are no longer in her home watching herself flirt with Lucas.

Jacque looks around and realizes immediately where they are. "This is Jen's room."

The Great Luna simply nodded and looked at the door of Jen's bedroom which suddenly flew open with a loud thud as it hit the wall.

"I've had it!" Jen snapped as she stomped into the room. She pulled her phone out of her back pocket and tapped the screen a few times before putting it to her ear. "Sally, she's done it again," Jen yelled without bothering to say hello. "We were supposed to have a girls night, hang out, and do our nails and all that crap. And what does little Jacquelyn Pierce do? She texts me, TEXTS me, Sally, that she forgot that she'd already made plans with Lucas." Jen sneered the name as if it were a toxic waste she was talking about and not a person.

Jen listens to Sally, all the while nodding her head ferociously. "I know. I know. Girl you aren't telling me anything. We both told her that if she didn't cut this crap out we were going to take matters into our own hands. They've been dating for four months and he's like a freaking baby cat attached to its mother's teat. Yes, dammit, I said 'teat.' That's not the point, Sal. The point is there is something not natural about the guy. He gives me the heebee jeebees."

Jacque was speechless, not that they could hear her even if she did have words. How could she possibly be dating Lucas

Steele? How could she pick him over her friends? Even with Fane, her friends were still mega important and he totally understood that.

More nodding was coming from Jen as she was apparently listening to Sally give a similar opinion of the situation. "I'm thinking a major intervention is in order," Jen barked into the phone. "I'm talking full blown, tie that bitch up, and drag her away from him so that we can talk some sense into her." Jen was pacing the room like a mad woman, her hand clenching and unclenching at her side. Jacque hadn't seen her friend that mad since Decebel decided it was his duty to die for their child.

Again Jen was listening intently to Sally on the other end of the phone. This time she added grunting and cat-like hissing sounds to her continued nodding. "Oh, don't even get me started on the secrets she's keeping," the blonde suddenly spat. "She thinks we don't know her well enough to know when she is hiding something from us? I swear he's doing voodoo on her or something. When has our red-headed friend ever, EVER, not told us everything? I mean our whole friendship has always been based on full disclosure. It's like in the best friend code of conduct or some crap like that. Best friends don't let best friends drive into stupid boyfriend situations." She paused, listening to Sally again. "Exactly. I say we ambush her at like four in the morning. If that's the only time we can get her alone, then so be it. Operation knock some bloody sense into our red-headed friend who's got her head shoved so far up her butt she doesn't even smell a rotten douche bag when he's standing right in front of her is now under way. Yes, yes, I know that's a ridiculously long name. Sue me, I get wordy when I'm pissed. K bye."

She jerked the phone away from her ear and tossed it on her bed. Jacque continued to watch the Jen from the past pace while muttering under her breath. It sickened her to think that she had caused this. She'd put a rift in their relationship for a guy that wasn't even her soul mate.

"She loves you," the Great Luna said placing a hand on Jacque's shoulder. "That is why she is so angry, because she loves you and wants what's best for you." Once again they are pulled from the room but this time when they stop Jacque doesn't recognize her surroundings.

"I've never been—" she begins but her words get stuck in her lungs as she watches Lucas carry her into the room. He tosses her playfully onto a large bed and she giggles.

"I do not sound like that when I laugh," Jacque snarled as she watched herself smile up at him. She wanted to walk across the room and smack the grin off of her own face.

"I really need to get home. If I break curfew my mom will make me work every weekend from now until I graduate," the past Jacque said still smiling like an idiot.

Lucas let out a low sigh. "Our time together goes too fast." He laid down beside her and played with a tendril of her hair. Lucas stared at her with such intensity that Jacque nearly had to look away from them, and when he leaned forward she understood clearly that he was going to kiss the Jacque laying with him.

"Please don't make me watch," Jacque pleaded as she placed a hand on the Great Luna's arm. "Please." She closed her eyes and when she opened them again she was back in her room. Her eyes widened as she looked at the three girls standing next to Jacque's bed.

"I guess this is the intervention?" Jacque looked over at the Great Luna.

"You three friends have a rare blessing in each other. You don't find such devotion in many relationships." The Great Luna turned back to the group.

"We're doing this for your own good, Jacque," Jen told the Jacque standing in front of her. "You haven't been yourself since you started dating that best friend thief and we're tired of it."

"Lucas isn't the problem," her past self responded.

"Are you implying that we are the problem?" Sally asked pressing a hand to her chest.

"Look, I know that I've been spending a lot of time with him, and I've canceled on you guys a couple of times."

"A couple of times?" Jen scoffed. "Are you living in an alternate reality or something, Red? Try every time for the past two months. You are with him constantly. You don't return our calls. You text us when you want to cancel instead of growing a pair and looking us in the face when you bail. I don't even know who you are anymore. And don't even get me started on the crap we know that you aren't telling us."

Jacque watched as the face of her past self paled. So she was keeping something from them.

"Now you're just letting your vivid imagination fill your head full of crap, Jennifer," the other Jacque huffed as she folded her arms across her chest. "I have no secrets. And I honestly don't mean to blow y'all off. Lucas can just be really persuasive."

"I frankly don't give a damn if Lucas pee's gold and craps twenty dollar bills. He's making you keep things from your best friends and that is not cool, Jac. Not. Cool." Jen looked as though she might reach across the bed and strangle her best friend.

The past Jacque stood there staring at her two friends and, after several minutes of tense silence, she seemed to deflate as if all the air had been let out of her. "They aren't my secrets to tell, Jen."

"Maybe not, but it was your lie. You could have just told us instead of lying to us about it all together." Jen's voice was full of hurt. Her shoulders slumped forward as she shook her head. "I know you think he's perfect, but he's not good for you, Red. Why can't you see that?"

"How can you possibly know what's good for me when you won't even take the time to get to know him?"

"Excuse me?" Sally jumped in. "We tried, but if you can recall, your precious Lucas was a complete and total ass to us the couple of times that we were with you guys. And you just made excuses for him. He'd had a bad day, or he just doesn't share well, or blah, blah, blah. Don't you dare lay that on us."

"You know what?" Jen asked as she met the past Jacque's hard gaze. "I'm done. If you can't see the truth when it's slapping you in your stupid face, then I'm not going to waste my oxygen on you. When you realize that Lucas Steele is not who he seems to be and come running back to us, you had better hope I'm in one of my forgiving moods."

Both Jacque's snorted, though the girls only heard one of them. The past Jacque added, "You don't have forgiving moods."

Jen turned for the door with Sally on her heels. "Then I guess your screwed, Red. Have a nice life."

The bedroom door closed behind them and it was as if a prison door had been slammed shut and Jacque was on the wrong side of it. She watched her past self slide to the floor as the realization of what had just happened fell heavily on her shoulders. Her body shook as she tried to hold in the tears.

"I'm an idiot," Jacque whispered to the Great Luna as her own heart broke right along with her former self.

"You were blinded by a charming, handsome man who caught you at a vulnerable time after Trent broke up with you. The most difficult thing in this whole situation is that though Lucas' good intentions will only have ill effects, he genuinely cares for you."

"Can we go?" Jacque asked her as she watched the past her fall apart. She didn't want to hear about how a wolf that wasn't her mate cared for her, especially when that relationship was tearing her friendships apart.

The Great Luna looked over at her and nodded. "Perhaps, now is a good time to show you how your true mate fares without you by his side."

Jacque's stomach dropped. She truly hoped she wasn't about to have to watch Fane with another girl the way she'd just watched herself with Lucas.

"What if I tell you that I've seen the error of my ways? Can we just go back to our time?"

The Great Luna smiled as she took Jacque's hand. "I want to believe you, but it is my experience that humans never learn that quickly, and you, my child, are half human."

Jacque attempted to steel herself against what she might see. She didn't know if she could watch Fane have a life without her. In fact, she was pretty sure that if she watched Fane smile at another female the way she'd just watched herself smile at Lucas she might attempt to claw the chick's eyes out. Wouldn't that be dignifying?

Chapter 7

Fane and Decebel ran through the forest, and though they weren't in their wolf forms, they still moved inhumanly fast. Fane had caught Jacque's scent the minute he'd gotten out of the SUV, which had been about the same time Decebel finally decided to tell him that his mate and Jen were being chased by wild boar. He kept trying to reach out to her, but she had their mental bond closed up tight. All he could picture was his pregnant mate running through a dark forest with pigs attempting to trample her. She wasn't helpless, by any means, but she was his and she was once again in harms' way.

"How far did Jen say they were?" Fane asked Decebel as the Alpha kept pace beside him.

"She didn't," he growled. "She was yelling like a maniac and then she just shut me out."

Fane was pretty sure that they would never fully understand their females. They wanted space, of course, but all hell would break loose if the males were the ones who closed the bonds. They wanted open and honest feelings, and yet Jacque hid from him instead of talking to him about whatever it was that had caused *her* to close their bond. He was truly at a loss on how to be what she needed.

Decebel suddenly made a sharp turn as he yelled, "There!"

Fane altered his course to follow the Alpha. He'd lost Jacquelyn's trail a quarter of a mile back and could only pick up Jen's scent and the scent of wild pigs. But still he kept running because Jen had said they were together. He had no reason to believe that Jen would be lying about it.

Jen continued to run despite the fact that she could feel her mate closing in on her. For someone who prided herself on her adaptability, she was feeling rather unprepared. She was blaming it on pregnancy hormones… No, not her own, she couldn't get by with that anymore but she could claim Jacque's. "Yeah, you just keep telling yourself that, blondie," she grumbled to herself as she pushed her feet to move even faster. Jen knew she wasn't going to keep it up much longer. Decebel was simply just too much stronger and faster than her. His legs were more powerful and able to cover more ground than hers, no matter how much she hated to admit it.

When she could hear his breathing behind her, she knew it was time to move on to part two of her plan...whatever the hell that was. She slowed down until she was able to come to a stop and leaned over, resting her hands on her knees. Her breathing was fast, but she was in no way out of breath. Werewolves could run for a long time before they finally gave out.

Decebel's arms were around her seconds later and she leaned into his touch as she always did and always would. Jen was going to soak it up while she could because it wouldn't be long before he put on his brooding face and started grilling her with questions that she was not going to have answers to.

"Are you alright?" he asked, his voice low and fervent.

Jen pulled back to look up at him and sure enough his amber eyes glowed with the presence of his wolf. "I'm good."

"Where is Jacquelyn?" Fane asked as she watched him stomp around in useless circles searching through the trees. Jen could tell he was trying to listen as well. Poor wolf wouldn't hear what he was hoping to.

"Okay, so you might want to sit down for this," Jen said as she stepped out of Decebel's hold. She pulled the band from her hair and re-gathered it into a neater pony tail, more to stall than for any other reason. It wasn't like she really cared what she looked like in that moment.

"No offense, Jen, but I don't want to sit. I want to see my mate. Is she alright? Has she found a place to hide from the boar?" Fane's eyes were glowing the ice blue that was freaky as much as it was beautiful.

Jen let out a long sigh. Damn, she hated to give in so easily, but what was she supposed to do? It's not like she could just keep running and expecting them to follow her. Eventually both the males were going to figure out that there weren't any stupid pigs in the forest and there sure as hell wasn't any Jacque. "Okay, so it's like this," she began. "I came over here with every intention of spending some time with my bestie and hoping to figure out what's crawled up her butt and made her act so weird. When I got here I caught her scent leading into the forest. It was strong so I knew it was recent." Jen paused and wondered if maybe she should skip all the truly unnecessary information, because Fane was really starting to look a tad crazy. But then she remembered the Great Luna asking her to distract him. She couldn't let the deity down, so the long, totally unnecessary version it would be.

"So what did I do?" she asked as she walked over to a tree and leaned up against it, crossing her arms in front of her chest— might as well get comfortable. "I trek my happy little butt up into the forest, in the dark, where it is beginning to get cold. The whole time I'm marching along I'm thinking my pregnant little friend—well not little. . .because let's face it, the girl's butt has expanded. Anyways, I'm thinking she better have brought something warm to wear, because as you can see," she said as she pointed to herself, "I did not come prepared to take a leisurely stroll through the cold mountain terrain. But then, knowing Jacque, and what a planner she is not, I'm figuring she probably didn't put on a coat so I started to pick up the pace. I didn't realize how far I'd gone until I happen to look around and notice all the big boulders and crevices in the mountain. This is where you," she said looking at Decebel, "contacted me about my breathing. Truth be told, babe, I was having some flashbacks to a certain time when a nut job pushed me into one of those crevices."

Decebel growled and took a step toward here. Jen held up her hand. "Chill, big guy, I lived. I'm here. It's all good." Jen had yet to open the bond completely back up, and she felt Decebel's very powerful push and finally dropped it.

"Are you truly okay?" he asked and the tone of his voice had her wanting to crawl up in his lap and reassure him that memories weren't enough to have her falling apart.

"I'm fine, B. It just caught me by surprise."

He watched her intently before finally nodding.

"Not to interrupt but could you please just get to the part where you tell me where Jacquelyn is?" Fane asked and Jen could tell he was trying very hard to keep the growl out of his voice.

"Right," Jen said turning back to him. "So, after dealing with that minor setback I continued on my mission to figure out where Jacque was and why the crap she'd gone so far into the mountains at night."

Fane paused in his pacing and closed his eyes. *Okay, Jen,* she thought, *maybe I should tone it down about his mate being alone in the dark cold mountains full of predators.*

"Maybe you should just get to the point," her mate helpfully added.

She shot him a glare. *"I have a reason for doing what I'm doing."*

"Naturally," he huffed.

"Not too long after the boulders, I picked up a scent that didn't belong in the forest."

Fane's head snapped around and his eyes narrowed on her.

Jen held up a hand. "Whoa, hold it together a little longer wolf-man. It was the Great Luna." Jen inwardly growled at herself for not having a better plan. Man, it was embarrassing to have to resort to the truth, especially since giving him the truth wasn't really going to help. Regardless of what the

Great Luna had told her, she still didn't have a clue where Jacque was, and that was not going to make the already pissed off wolf any happier.

"What did she say?" Fane practically snarled.

Decebel took several steps closer to his mate; his natural instinct to protect her, no matter who it was, taking over. Jen knew she was going to have to tread carefully. Male werewolves were touchy about their females on a good day. Fane did not know where his mate was and could not communicate with her. It definitely wasn't a good day.

"You know how she can be," Jen hedged. "She said a whole lot but very little of it was any use. Basically, it was a whole lot of Jacque needing to learn a lesson about something—blah, blah, blah— and she might have mentioned something about needing me to distract you for a bit so that she would have time to teach Jacque said lesson. So naturally because she is a deity and all and could basically zap my ass out of existence if she wanted to, I did as I was told and I provided a distraction. I will admit that it was not my best effort, but, seriously, look at what I had to work with." She motioned to the forest around her. "I'm honestly quite ashamed that I've had to give you this long, drawn out story, though it is the truth, when I could have just told you that last part. But you have to try and understand the position that I'm in here, Fane. I mean surely if the Great Luna knows where Jacque is then she isn't in any danger." Jen was attempting to sound reasonable but judging by the rapid breathing that was issuing forth from Fane, he was a few exits past reasonable-ville.

"So where did she say my mate was?" Fane asked and his words sounded a tad garbled since his incisors had lengthened— not a good sign.

Jen chuckled. "Funny thing that, um." She paused. "She didn't exactly say."

"So she gave you an idea of where she is?" Fane asked, his piercing blue eyes boring into her.

"Not so much." Jen shook her head.

Fane was shaking with the need to phase, to hunt, and to protect his mate. Jen knew exactly what he was going through because she'd felt those emotions running through her own mate when she and their daughter had been in danger. He was basically a ticking time bomb. And here she thought things were going to be all calm and hunky dory for once. That will teach her to think.

Chapter 8

The world around Fane suddenly disappeared as his tunnel vision set in. All he could see was his pregnant mate, in his mind's eye, surrounded by every possible danger he could think of. He had no idea where she was or how to find her. He wanted to believe that if the Great Luna was involved, then his mate had to be safe, but that just wasn't enough for him. He needed to see her or, at the very least, hear her voice. He was beginning to realize that everything he'd been upset about, all the things he couldn't move past, really amounted to a huge pile of nothing that, through his own self-pity, he had made into a big deal.

For the past few months, he should have been enjoying the time with his mate instead of fretting over the past. He should have been relishing the moments they had without danger constantly knocking at their door. Instead of worrying about his ability to protect his child, or whether or not he would make a good father, he should have been rejoicing that they were even expecting a child considering how difficult it was for their kind to have children. Fane had squandered the time they'd had and now he didn't have either his mate or his child. Why did it always take drastic measures to make him see what was right in front of his face?

Focus on her, his wolf spoke up, obviously losing patience with the man. *Let us get her back and then you will fix the wrong.* It was one of those moments when Fane was truly thankful for his beast and his ability to think without the cloud of emotions hanging over him.

We will search for her, Fane told him. He felt his wolf's agreement but wasn't prepared for the sudden phase that his beast forced. One minute he was standing on two legs and the next his clothes were shredded and he was on all fours. Everything around him sharpened into focus as all of his wolf's senses took over.

"Are you alright, Fane?" Decebel's voice had his large wolf head turning to look at the Alpha.

Fane met his eyes for several seconds before nodding and dropping them. He turned back to look deeper into the forest, and despite his inability to scent her, it was the only direction he knew to go so he took off at a sprint, unworried about what Decebel and Jen would do. They weren't his concern. Only Jacquelyn and their pup mattered. As he ran, he drew comfort from the memories—the times when he had allowed himself to enjoy her. He let them pour over him until he was drenched in her presence even though she wasn't with him.

He remembered the night that she fell apart in his arms because she felt unattractive. A smile pulled at his wolf's lips as the memory filled him.

"*You have been distant today,*" Fane sent through their bond as he walked into their bedroom after having spent some time training with some of the other wolves. He glanced around the room and saw that Jacque wasn't there, but he knew she was close. His eyes landed on the closed bathroom door and he frowned.

"Jacquelyn?" he called as he walked over to the door and tried turning the knob. It was locked. He let out a deep growl. "Open the door, love." It was then that her emotions hit him rocking him back on his heels. She was hurting. "Luna, open the door," he said more urgently. He heard the sniffling of tears and felt her move closer to the door until he knew she was just on the other side of it.

"I don't want you to see me," she practically whispered.

"I'm sorry to have to be the one to tell you, but you are all I want to see. I'm thirsty for the sight of you. Please, open the door." Fane held his palm against the door as he closed his eyes and tried to search her mind for what was bothering her. Her emotions were a mess—all tangled up in fear, anxiety, self-doubt, and frustration.

She laughed, but it wasn't a humorous sound. It was tinged with a bit of hysteria. "I wanted to surprise you tonight. Jen talked me into getting something special to wear and, like the fool I am, I did it."

Fane's pulse sped up a little as he imagined all of the times in the past that his mate had surprised him like that. He thoroughly enjoyed the sight of her in anything, but Jacquelyn in lingerie was something that drove him crazy. He let her feel his passion and excitement. Apparently, that was the wrong thing to do.

She slammed her hand against the door and her anger ran over him in a violent wave. "I don't look like that!" she snarled at him. He hadn't realized how he'd been picturing her. Okay, so he'd just learned a valuable lesson—do not picture his mate in her pre-pregnant state unless the bond is thoroughly and completely closed.

"You're right; you don't. You are even more beautiful now," he said gently as he tried the knob again. He was going to wind up breaking the damn thing if she didn't let him in very soon.

Jacquelyn snorted. "What's beautiful about me, Fane? The stretch marks, the dimples, the protruding belly, or, perhaps, it's the lovely emotions that seemed to be all over the damn place that make me such a pleasant person to be around. Tell me, mate of mine, EXACTLY WHAT IS IT THAT TURNS YOU ON?"

Fane should have stayed calm. He should have talked her down but she had locked herself away from him. She was angry, feeling insecure and desperate for him, and yet she wouldn't let him near her. So calm is not what he stayed.

"YOU!" His voice echoed through the room at the same time his palm hit the door rattling it in its frame. "YOU ARE WHAT TURN ME ON. Don't you get that? I hide nothing from you, Jacquelyn. My mind is open to you; don't you see the way I see you?" He was pleading with her to trust him, to trust not just his words but his actions. Maybe he hadn't paid enough attention to her; maybe that was why she was feeling so undesirable.

"You can hide things from me," Jacquelyn whispered. "You know as well as I do that if there is something we don't want the other to know, that it's possible to keep it locked away. Just go, Fane. Leave me alone until I can be rational."

Fane roared. He might has well have been a lion instead of a wolf. He didn't turn to look when their bedroom door flew open and Jen's voice broke through his own.

"What the hell, Fane?" Jen snapped. "We thought there was something serious going on."

"Jennifer Anghelesco, you are a dead woman!" Jacquelyn yelled through the door.

"What did I do?" Jen huffed. "I just heard your maniac mate growling like a rabies infested beast and came in to make sure everyone was okay."

Fane turned to glare at the Alpha female. "You told her to buy—" He had to stop because his canines were growing making it difficult for him to talk. His head swung back around when he heard the bathroom door open.

Jacquelyn stood there wrapped up in a robe, tears streaking her face. "You told me to buy that damn lingerie! That's why."

Fane was moving for the door but she was faster and slammed it right in his face turning the lock back in place.

"Did you criticize her in her pregnant state?" Jen asked him accusingly. "Because I will castrate you if you did. I mean, Fane, I know you wolves can be dense but surely even you have enough sense not to say something negative about your mate, especially when she's carrying around your child in her body."

Fane heard Decebel join his mate and he was so very glad that he'd shown up. "Decebel, please remove your mate from my presence."

"WHAT!" Jen stomped her foot. "I am not going until I know my best friend is alright!"

"Jennifer, you should know better than to interfere with a male and his mate," Decebel told her quietly. "He won't hurt her. You know all he wants is to make her happy. Now let's go before he loses what little control he has."

"You had better make this right, Fane Lupei. I don't give a hot poker in hell if it's your fault or not. You put a smile back on my Jacque's face or so help me…" Jen's words trailed off as Fane heard the door close.

He stood in the middle of the room attempting to hold his wolf back. His beast was snarling at him, urging him to get to her. She'd told them to leave but there was no way he or his wolf would do as she commanded. Fane turned back to look at the thin piece of wood that stood sentry between him and the woman he loved. Never had a door looked so offensive as in that moment.

He walked purposefully over to it and no longer willing to grant her the privacy she apparently wanted, he turned the knob until the lock broke. Fane pushed the door open slowly and stepped into the bathroom. He found her on the floor next to the large tub, the robe still wrapped around her and her forehead leaning on the cold porcelain edge.

When he started to walk toward her, Jacquelyn held up her hand and shook her head at him. "Please don't. Just let me be." Her voice shook with her tears.

Fane ignored her plea and reached down to pick her up. When she started to push him away his wolf decided to make an appearance and Fane knew his eyes would be glowing a fierce blue. "Mate," his beast snarled, "do not. You might hurt yourself."

Jacquelyn looked up at him then, meeting his gaze. "You wouldn't understand; you're just a wolf."

His wolf leaned closer to her, pressing his nose against her neck and breathing in her scent—a scent that brought him comfort and peace and also drove him insane. "I may be just a wolf, female, but I am your wolf and you are mine. Do not ever ask us to leave you when you need us most."

Fane carried her into their room and forced his wolf to let the man have control once more. He sat with his mate in his lap and brushed the hair away from her face. "Jacquelyn, look at me," he commanded gently.

She didn't.

"Look at me," Fane repeated slower.

Finally she let out a resigned sigh and raised her head so that her green eyes met his.

"Don't ever ask me to leave you when you are so upset." She started to say something but he placed a finger over her lips. "Hear me. Every instinct I have is to protect, love, and cherish you. For you to ask me to walk away while you are in pain, be it emotional or physical, is cruel."

"Not to mention futile," she muttered quickly earning her a nip on the neck from him.

"I am sorry that you feel inadequate, Luna. You are anything but. I will tell you with my words so that you can hear me. But know this mate, before this night is over I will show you so that you have no doubt just how attractive I find you."

She shook her head at him but again he ignored her.

"I have found you desirable from the moment I laid eyes on you. The attraction has only grown in intensity the longer we have been together. My need for you grows with every touch, every taste, and every time you give yourself to me. I thought I would need you less once the need had been satisfied but the opposite is true. I only need and want you more. And now, my beautiful Luna, you carry my child inside of you." His hand slipped between the opening of the robe and pressed gently against her rounded stomach. "Your face radiates the joy that I feel. Whether you believe it or not, I have loved every change that has happened to your incredible body." Fane tugged down the shoulder of the robe and nipped her again when she started to argue. "No," he scolded. "You don't get to tell me how I feel or how I see you. I see every stretch mark as a beauty mark that tells the story of how you created a precious life. Everything that you see as negative, I see as evidence of just how incredible you are. I love every single inch of you and there is nothing, especially not carrying my child, that could change that."

"I didn't realize how vain I am," Jacque said quietly. "But when compared to you, with your perfect werewolf body and chiseled features, I just feel like a big blob."

Fane stood up and placed her feet on the floor. She started to protest but he was having none of it. "Shh," he soothed as he untied the robe she'd been hiding under. "Look at me, Jacquelyn. Look at my face and nowhere else." His hands shook as he pushed the robe from her shoulders. "You are even more beautiful than the first time I removed a robe from you." His voice was soft, but he knew she could hear the awe that filled him as he took her in.

Fane took her small face in his hands and brushed his thumb across her lips. He had tasted them at least a hundred times and yet he was still starved for them, for her. When he raised his eyes to meet hers, he used their bond to convey an image to her of how he saw her.

"No," Jacquelyn whispered as she attempted to shake her head.

"Yes," Fane argued before pressing his lips to hers. As his hands slid down her neck and then shoulders and finally rested on her hips, he pulled her tighter against him, bunching the sheer fabric in his fists. There was no doubt that the lingerie was beautiful, but now that he'd seen it, it was only a hindrance to the package beneath. And like the precious gift that she was, Fane unwrapped her, slowly—piece by piece—making sure that she could feel through their bond just what she did to him. Over and over he kissed, touched, and loved her body reverently.

Sometime later, back in their bed, he pressed his lips to her bare belly and kissed her gently. The growl that rumbled out of him was straight from his wolf. "Mine." Fane's grip on her hips tightened as he pressed his face against her flesh. Her warmth, her scent, and her taste surrounded him and he was drunk on her.

"Yes, we are yours," Jacquelyn agreed.

Fane's eyes crawled up her body to stare into her eyes. "Don't ever doubt me again," he whispered before leaning down and kissing her on the neck where his mark was.

Fane shook himself as the memory faded away leaving him feeling empty. He needed to find her now. He needed to know that she was alright and that their baby was alright. Fane threw his head back and let out a deep, mournful howl, pouring all of his fear into it. He longed to hear her answer him, but as the sound died away, he was left with a silence that pierced him to his soul.

"Peace, wolf,." The voice in his mind did not belong to his mate, but it had him coming to a sudden stop anyway.

"I will not let any harm come to her," the Great Luna assured him.

"Where is she?" Fane tried very hard not to growl.

"She is where she needs to be at this moment."

And just as quickly as her presence had come, she was gone. Fane knew it was futile, but he did it anyway. Desperation making him willing to try anything, he reached through their bond but found that it was still locked up tight.

"Please let me in, Jacquelyn." He was at a complete loss as to what to do. His wolf needed action and so once again he headed deeper into the mountain unwilling to give up looking for her until she was with him, where she belonged.

Chapter 9

Jacque's gut clenched as she and the Great Luna appeared before the doors of the Romanian pack mansion. Part of her wanted to fling the door open and run inside because she was so desperate for the sight of her mate. The other part of her was too scared to move. What if, in that alternate reality, he'd found someone else?

"What if I can't handle what I see?" Jacque asked the goddess.

"You do not have a choice," she answered. "There are times in life when it is necessary to see the whole truth to fully understand the weight of a decision before it is made. Such a time is this." The Great Luna waved toward the doors and they opened.

Jacque hesitated briefly before finally following the goddess inside. Everything looked the same, yet she knew immediately that it was different somehow. The air felt heavy, weighted down with despair and darkness. They continued walking further into the mansion and Jacque recognized the door to the study. The Great Luna motioned for her to enter the room. *What was she going to say? 'No thank you, I think I'll pass? Not likely,* Jacque thought as she walked into Vasile's study, a room she'd been in many, many times, and yet it had never been filled with such darkness.

Decebel stood to her far right. His large arms crossed in front of his chest with his brooding frown firmly in place. He looked like a stranger to her. Shadows seemed to wrap around him and the very light in the room seem to avoid him.

Vasile was sitting on one of the loveseats; his eyes were tired and his mouth pulled into a tight line. He looked older, though he still didn't have grey hair or any wrinkles. She heard footsteps behind her and watched as Sorin and then Fane walked into the room.

Jacque took a step toward her mate but stopped when she remembered that he couldn't see her. She ached with the need to feel his arms around her and to have him tell her that everything would be fine, that he would never let her go, and that he loved her. None of those things had ever been in doubt, but that did not mean she needed to hear them any less.

She watched as he took a seat next to his father. His blue eyes held no tenderness in them. They were as hard as the marble tile upon which she now stood.

"You've been graduated for a year now, Fane," Vasile spoke, breaking the silence.

Jacque looked over at the Great Luna. The goddess nodded. "Yes, this is two years after you should have met him."

Jacque turned back to the men and watched as Fane clenched and unclenched his jaw. "I'm not ready."

"What kind of answer is that?" Vasile snapped. "You told me two years ago that you felt like you needed to go to the U.S. but that you weren't sure you were ready. I understood then because you were young. You are a pup no longer. If you feel a pull to go, then you know what it could mean."

"But we know there are no packs in that area. That's the whole reason I backed out the first time. Why on earth would my mate be in Cold Spring, Texas where there are no Canis lupus?" Fane argued. "Besides, don't you think we have bigger things to worry about?"

That had Jacque perking up even more.

Vasile shrugged. "Desdemona makes her threats; we've been holding her off. She will still be here when we return. Now back to your first question. It doesn't matter if you can't explain it. We are werewolves and for all intents and purposes should not exist, yet we do. You need a mate." Vasile motioned toward Decebel. "He needs a mate. Hell, half the pack needs mates, and they haven't found any here. Maybe you are to be the catalyst for something good, Fane."

"So you're telling me that if I don't go then I'm responsible for the other males not finding their mates?" Fane's eyes narrowed on his father.

"I simply want to know what you're afraid of."

Fane stood from his spot and walked over to the fireplace. There were no flames in its hearth, which only served to make the room seem colder. His shoulders were tense and Jacque wished she could ease his frustration.

"I just have a feeling that I'm not going to like what I find," he answered finally.

Jacque knew she shouldn't be offended because she didn't think he meant that he wouldn't like her, but it still stung.

"You don't think you will like your mate?" Sorin spoke up for the first time.

Fane shook his head in frustration. "No, that's not what I mean. I mean something is wrong."

"I would think that if something is wrong and your mate might be involved it would be all the more reason to go." Decebel's deep voice sounded foreign to Jacque's ears. There was no warmth in it. Like his dead eyes, his voice was lifeless.

"We're going," Vasile said as he stood up briskly. "As your Alpha, I'm telling you that we are going. Decebel, Sorin, and Costin will join us. We are going to lay this to rest once and for all. Get your stuff packed and meet at the vehicle in twenty minutes." Vasile stormed from the room leaving behind a very frustrated Fane, surprised Sorin, and unmoving Decebel.

"Why do you want to go?" Fane turned to face Decebel.

Decebel's amber eyes looked at Fane and for a second Jacque saw them flash with the glow of the wolf. "I honestly don't know. I've given up on finding a true mate. I don't deserve one. But like a blister being rubbed over and over, I'm raw with the need to act. My wolf is more restless than he's ever been, and the only thing that seems to calm him is the idea of going with you to this Cold Spring place."

"And what if you do find your mate there? What if you don't like what you find?"

A wicked grin that was similar to the ones Jacque had seen on Decebel's face before took the place of his frown. But unlike the wicked grins she'd seen, this one lacked any emotion. "Then I will kill him."

Fane's mouth dropped open briefly before he caught himself. "So if you find your female and she's already with someone then you…" Fane's words trailed off.

Decebel nodded. "Yes, then I'd take care of it. Though I do not feel I deserve a mate, my instincts would never allow me to walk away from her if I found her, and I sure as hell wouldn't leave her in the hands of another male."

Jacque wasn't surprised by Decebel's words, but she was surprised at how cold they sounded.

"Is that what you think you will find?" Sorin asked Fane having stood up and walked toward the door.

Fane nodded. "I should have gone when I felt prompted the first time, but I just couldn't rationalize as to why America or why Texas. My gut tells me she's there, but she's no longer alone."

Jacque's stomach dropped to her toes as she realized what was about to happen. She didn't feel the Great Luna's hand on her arm or even notice the pull and empty space as they traveled. All she could think about was that Fane was coming to find her, two years after it should have happened, and he was going to find her with Lucas.

"I think I'm going to be sick." Jacque slumped forward as the ground appeared beneath her feet. She stumbled forward but was caught by the goddess' hand. She didn't have time to recover or to prepare herself.

"Why are you here?" Lucas' voice rumbled through the air.

Jacque straightened up and looked around her trying to get her bearings. She was standing in her front yard and, to her surprise, Jen and Sally were there.

"I thought they left me?" Jacque asked the goddess.

"Did you think your friends would ever really abandon you for good? They were always destined to be a part of my children. Since you and Fane did not meet at the designated time, the Fates had to make sure that they would be in the right place at the next opportunity for their own destinies to become fulfilled. Jen and Sally both are dating wolves from Lucas' pack."

"Do they know what they are?" Jacque asked as she looked at Jen who was standing next to a handsome, blonde guy.

"Yes, which is partly why they forgave you. They realized it must have been difficult to keep such a secret.

"I need to speak with you." Fane's voice drew her attention and when she looked at him she saw that he wasn't answering Lucas' question, he was talking to her—well, her other self. Jacque looked at the face of the future Jacque and could see clearly the confusion and shock in her eyes. Future Jacque tilted her head to the side as she stared back at Fane, and she knew that he must be using their bond to talk.

"Huh, I do make funny faces when we talk through the bond," she mused as she continued to watch the drama unfold in front of her.

"She is mine," Lucas snarled.

Fane looked away from future Jacque then and his face was strangely calm. When he met Lucas' eyes, he almost looked amused. "Are you sure about that?"

"She's been mine for two years."

Fane took a step toward the Cold Spring Alpha. "Does she bear your mark? Does she wear markings that match your own?" Fane's voice had dropped low as he challenged the other male. "Does she hear your voice in her mind?"

Future Jacque looked up at Lucas and the doubts were already beginning to slip through the cracks that Fane was putting in the carefully crafted reality that Lucas had built.

"If she doesn't bear your mark, then Fane has every right to challenge you." Vasile stepped up next to his son.

"Who are you?" Lucas asked through narrowed eyes.

" 'Who are you?' is a more appropriate question," Vasile parried. "You see, I am the

Alpha of the Romanian pack, and I know *all* the other Alphas. But I don't know you and you are not on any pack roster. Who are you, Lucas Steele, and why do you have an unregistered pack?"

Lucas tried to meet Vasile's eyes but couldn't. Jacque —the Jacque who was watching in horrid fascination—knew that Lucas wasn't nearly dominant enough to hold Vasile's gaze. Then again, few could stand against her father-in-law.

"Do you accept my challenge?" Fane asked, his eyes staring at future Jacque.

"I accept," Lucas growled as he took future Jacque's hand.

"She will not stay with you," Vasile spoke up. "You know the rules of the challenge. You will remain separated from her until after the challenge."

"Do I have a say in this?" Future Jacque finally seemed to snap out of her shocked state.

"No," all three males responded.

She turned her glare on Fane and once again her eyes took on that faraway look. Jacque was actually jealous of her future self as the other got to speak to Fane through their bond for the first time. She missed her mate and missed that connection.

Just when Jacque thought they would be walking away from that encounter without bloodshed, at least until the challenge, Decebel walked across the lawn passing Vasile and Fane until he was standing about ten feet from Jen and the male with her.

"Decebel," Vasile warned.

Jacque saw the claws on his hands then and realized why the Alpha was growling at his Beta. Decebel was barely in control of his wolf.

"I challenge for her," he said in a voice barely understandable.

Jen's eye narrowed as she looked from the guy next to her back to Decebel. "Excuse me, Tarzan, but who the hell are you talking about?"

Jacque laughed out loud, glad that no one could hear her.

Decebel look at the guy standing next to Jen, but he couldn't even raise his head to look at Decebel. He was way outmatched. "Is this your—" Decebel paused and clenched his jaw so tight Jacque was sure his teeth would break at any minute. "Is this your—" he tried again.

"Dude, if it's that painful to talk then maybe you should just stop," Jen said, adding fuel to an already very volatile situation. "This is my boyfriend, if you must know."

Vasile walked over to where Decebel stood and placed a hand on his shoulder. "What is your name?" Vasile asked Jen.

"Jennifer Adams," she answered, though not with near as much attitude as she gave Decebel.

"You are human?"

"And you are not," Jen snorted. "Anything else we need to cover? Maybe we need to sort out what our genders are as well just for good measure?"

Jacque smacked a hand to her forehead. She looked over at future Jacque and that was when she noticed Sally standing next to another male. She turned quickly to look back at Sorin and Costin. Sure enough, Costin was eyeballing Sally like he hadn't eaten in about twenty years and she was a juicy T-bone.

She turned and looked at the Great Luna. "This is going to be a blood bath."

The Great Luna raised a brow at her. "It's a messy business trying to fix destiny when you step off the path designated for you."

"Decebel, are you sure?" Vasile asked and Jacque turned to look back at the group.

Decebel's eyes were glued to Jen and while Jen obviously appreciated the view, she wasn't about to swoon at his feet. *Some things never change,* Jacque thought.

"I challenge your boyfriend," Decebel growled, "for you."

Jen raised a single brow. "And what if I don't want you?"

Decebel took a step closer to her. The male next to her started to move but Decebel's head snapped up to look at him and the man fell to his knees. Guess it was blaringly obvious who was more dominant between the two.

Jen looked down at her boyfriend and then back up at Dec. Jacque grinned. Jen didn't want to admit it, she could tell, but she was impressed. No surprise there, she was Decebel's match in every way.

Decebel turned back to Jennifer and leaned in closer to her. He took a deep breath and Jacque saw his shoulders relax slightly.

"Are you going to answer my question?" Jen wiped the awed look off her face, obviously remembering that she was supposed to be irritated. "What if I don't want you?"

"You will," Decebel said softly.

Jen was speechless and, despite the circumstances, Jacque really wished she had a camera to capture the moment and show it to her friend once the nightmare was over.

Vasile watched his Beta for several more seconds before finally shaking his head. "So be it," he said and then turned back to Lucas. "Two challenges stand for two *unmarked* females you claim."

"So this is all happening because we don't have bite marks on our skin?" Jen spoke up stepping to the side of Decebel, being careful not to touch him, and faced Vasile.

"You are human and yet you know of our race. Have they not explained to you what it means to be a true mate?" Vasile asked her. "Did your boyfriend," (The word didn't sound like a good thing as he said it) "not tell you about what it meant to wear his mark or about your own markings that should match his? Did he not tell you about the bond between mates and the ability to communicate without words? Surely they've been open and honest with you about what it truly means to be mated to one such as us?"

Jen's jaw had dropped open but she quickly snapped it shut. "I'm sure they were going to get around to it, weren't you Lucas?" She spat at the Cold Spring Alpha.

Okay, Jacque thought, so maybe she'd forgiven Jacque, but it was obvious Jen still did not like Lucas.

"They haven't told us any of that." Sally's soft voice broke through the tense moment as she stepped up beside Jen.

Vasile's countenance softened immediately and Jacque wondered if he knew what she was.

Vasile bowed his head to her and pressed a hand over his heart. "Then I'm sure they have not bothered to tell you how precious you are, healer."

Yep, he knew.

"Alpha, you know how I hate to be left out of a good challenge." Costin's voice came from just behind her. He walked past Jacque, obviously unable to see her and straight toward Sally.

The grin on his face was all Costin—confident, cocky, and funny. But Jacque didn't miss the hostility lurking in his hazel eyes. Costin had not been unaffected by the two years without Sally.

Vasile let out a heavy sigh. "Who are you challenging for?"

Costin winked at Sally. "Brown eyes, do you have a male here who claims you?" he asked gently.

Sally seemed at a loss, so it was Jen who answered. "She's dating that one." Jen pointed to a short, stalky male with sandy brown hair and grey eyes. He was currently glaring daggers at Costin, but like the other males, he seemed unable to move.

Costin nodded to Jen. "Thank you. I challenge that one," he said and motioned toward the one Jen indicated, "for brown eyes."

"She has a name," Jen told him sharply.

Costin grinned, dimples and all. "I'm sure she does and I imagine it's as beautiful as she is. When she's ready she can whisper it to me."

Jen coughed as she looked from Costin to Sally. "Oh girl, he's good."

Sally blushed but still didn't say anything.

Vasile looked back at Sorin. "Do you want to challenge as well?"

Jacque could tell he was really hoping Sorin said no.

"I think I'll just watch," Sorin told his Alpha.

"Fine," Vasile turned back to Lucas. "You have your three challenges. Do I need to go over the rules or do you know them?"

"I know them."

Vasile nodded. "Good, here's my card." He handed Lucas a small, square piece of paper. "Call me in twelve hours with the location and time. The challenge must take place within three days of issuance."

As the group broke apart, Jacque watched her future self stare after Fane who was walking backward while staring at her. Lucas turned her to face him and Jacque could tell she was forcing herself to ignore Fane.

"So it doesn't matter what I do, we are still going to end up together?" Jacque asked the Great Luna as she watched her two best friends lead her future self into her house.

"You and Fane, like Jennifer and Decebel and Sally and Costin, were created for each other. After so many long years of darkness, you are the generation that must reunite my wolves. The supernatural world has been on the brink of self-destruction for quite some time. The division among them is weakening them, and the magic that has been in the human realm is fading. The fae have always held the supernatural races in check, but when they stepped back and hid away in Farie, they didn't realize the future consequences of their actions, not unlike someone else I know," she said narrowing her eyes on Jacque. "I realize that I have asked a lot of you and your companions and of my wolves. But it takes a spark to start a fire and you three ladies are my spark."

Chapter 10

"So is that it?" Jacque asked, waiting to see if the Great Luna would now take her back to the present.

"Not just yet. I think it is important that you see the consequences of your decisions. Though you may still end up with your mate, the consequences will be extreme. In your reality, when Fane challenged Lucas, they were the only two wolves that suffered the consequences. Lucas was the only wolf that forfeited his life. In this reality, that will not be the case. Not only will many more die but the risk of revealing yourselves to the human world becomes very real."

The Great Luna placed a hand on her shoulder and, in the blink of an eye, they were standing in Jacque's room. Jen, Sally, and Jacque were all in various sprawled positions, all looking a tad worse for wear.

"Okay, so a year and a half ago when you finally came clean about what Lucas was, I thought I'd seen it all," Jen said as she stared up at the ceiling fan as it rotated hypnotically. "I was so very, very wrong."

Future Jacque nodded. Her eyes were wide and she looked very lost. "I don't even know what to think."

"So that stuff that main guy was talking about, what was his name?" Jen thought for a minute. "Vasile." She snapped her fingers. "Yes, that was it. Was that stuff happening with you and the hottie who challenged Lucas? Were you able to hear his thoughts in your mind?"

Instead of answering future Jacque jumped up and jerked her shirt over her head.

"Okay, so just thinking about him has you so hot and bothered that you have to strip?" Jen asked as she sat up and watched her friend walk over to the mirror on her dresser.

Jacque hesitated before lifting her hair and turning so she could look over her shoulder. The breath whooshed from her body as her eyes took in the black, tattoo like markings that ran across her back from shoulder to shoulder.

Sally and Jen both stood and walked over to her. Their eyes were every bit as wide as future Jacque's.

Sally was next to strip off her shirt and turned to look over her shoulder, pulling her brown locks out of the way. She too had markings; only hers were down the center of her spine.

Jen took a step back. "For the first time, I really don't want to take my clothes off."

Future Jacque rolled her eyes at her blonde friend and then jerked Jen's shirt up. She turned her friend side to side looking her over. "There's nothing."

Jen let out a sigh. "Thank goodness for that. I thought I was going to be saddled to that cave man. I'm not saying he wasn't hotter than the seventh level of hell, but let's face it, his conversational skills need some serious work."

"You never answer her question," Sally said as she looked at future Jacque. "Could you hear his thoughts?"

Future Jacque nodded. "He apologized to me for making me wait."

"I heard that guy who challenged Eli in my mind,' Sally confirmed.

"You mean dimples?" Jen asked with a grin. "I bet he has girls falling at his feet begging him to let them lick those suckers."

Sally frowned. "You are so disturbed."

Jen shrugged. "There is nothing wrong with a good dimple licking if it happens to be on someone that looks like that wolf."

Future Jacque slipped her shirt back on and Sally did the same. Jen headed for the door as the other two took seats on the floor.

"This calls for hot chocolate. You two are looking a little pale and we obviously have strategy to discuss." She left the room, leaving Sally and future Jacque looking after her.

"She's taking this rather well," Sally pointed out.

Future Jacque nodded. "But then she took the 'whole werewolves are real' thing really well too."

"That was just because she finally realized why you were being so weird."

"True," future Jacque agreed.

"How do you think Lucas is doing?" Sally asked.

Future Jacque pinched the bridge of her nose and slowly shook her head from side to side. "I imagine he is just sort of blowing a gasket. You know he doesn't share well."

"Or at all," Sally added.

Jen was back several minutes later with a tray of coffee mugs and a package of Oreo cookies. "Okay, heifers, let's get serious," she said as she sat the tray down in the middle of their circle and took a seat. "What are we going to do if these. . .wait. . .what nationality are they? Russian?"

Future Jacque froze. Her breathing increased as her hands curled into tight fists. "Romanian," she finally said.

"Did he just tell you that using his mind mojo on you?" Jen asked.

She nodded.

"Man, this crap just keeps getting deeper and deeper," Jen muttered. "Okay, so what are we going to do if those Romanian wolves manage to win these challenges?"

Future Jacque looked at Sally. "Do you feel anything for Costin, the one who challenged for you?"

Sally paused before nodding. Her skin flushed as she took in a shaky breath. "It was like coming home," she whispered. "The minute he looked into my eyes I just wanted to walk into his arms. It was both unsettling and wonderful at the same time."

Future Jacque let out a small huff of laughter. "I don't think I could have put it better."

"Okay, hold up," Jen said leaning forward as her brow furrowed. "I will admit that the idea of throwing myself in Tarzan's arms definitely crossed my mind. But more than anything I just wanted to hit him in his too handsome, cocky face. I mean, I felt something, definitely a level of attraction that I've never felt before, but I wouldn't say that it was unsettling and wonderful. I'm going to go with more along the lines of volatile and possibly a little bit dirty."

Jacque laughed and smiled even wider when she saw the Great Luna smiling at Jen's comment. The girl always did have a way with words.

"Why do you think they called me a healer?" Sally asked before taking a sip of her hot chocolate.

Jen shrugged. "Beats the heck out of me. But it sounds like our men have been keeping quite a bit to themselves, which makes me just a tad perturbed."

"A tad?" Jacque and future Jacque said at the same time.

"Fine, it pisses me off. Happy?" Jen conceded.

"Being honest with yourself is an important—"

"Spare me the psychobabble, Florence," Jen growled.

"Florence Nightingale was a nurse, not a—" Sally started but was cut off by Jen again.

"Don't care. I told you when you started taking those classes that I didn't want you analyzing my every word or behavior."

"Speaking of classes," future Jacque interrupted. "When do yours start back?"

Sally and Jen both shrugged. "A couple of weeks. Summer gets shorter and shorter. I thought being in college meant longer breaks."

"Are you still taking this semester off?" Sally asked future Jacque.

Jacque looked at the Great Luna. "Why would I take the semester off?"

The Great Luna turned her gentle eyes on the redhead. "Your mom hasn't met Cypher. There are things you or your mother don't know about her gift. Back in our reality, she is just discovering that the magic that is part of her mate's people—the warlocks—has saved her from the ill effects that her gift can cause. But here, since she isn't exposed to that healing magic, over time her ability to sense things in people has grown stronger and is affecting her ability to function in normal everyday life. You chose to stay home to help her with the bookstore."

Jacque's mouth had gone dry and her stomach was turning into one big knot. How could so much be affected by one little choice? Her mom needed Cypher, just as she needed Fane. And Jacque would be taking that away from her if she went through with her plan and the Fates granted her request.

As day turned into night, Jacque and the Great Luna stayed, listening to the girls talk, speculate, and attempt to plan a future with all of the new information thrown at them. Jacque appreciated the goddess letting her spend time in their presence. She hadn't realized how much she'd missed them all being together. It was obvious, looking from the outside in, that they found energy and confidence and security in being with each other.

It was after midnight when future Jacque's phone rang. She looked at the screen and frowned. "It's Lucas."

"I can't believe he waited this long to call," Jen scoffed.

"He was probably trying to make sure those Romanian wolves weren't anywhere around," Sally pointed out.

Future Jacque answered it. "You're on speaker phone," she told him.

"Are you alright?" Lucas asked and it sounded as if he genuinely cared.

"I'm fine, Lucas, just a little confused,"

"Uh, try mega, freaking Disney World size confused," Jen cut in.

"Is everything they said true?" future Jacque asked.

"I want to talk to you about it, but not over the phone. We're down the street waiting for you three. I'm not going to let them keep us apart right before a challenge."

"Isn't that breaking the rules?" Sally asked.

Lucas chuckled. "When have I ever cared about rules when it came to my mate?"

Future Jacque frowned at the phone. "What will happen if they catch us?"

"Babe, trust me. It will be fine. I need to see you. Please come."

Jen rolled her eyes and make a gagging motion.

"Don't do it," Jacque muttered under her breath, though she knew they couldn't hear her.

"Okay we'll come," future Jacque acquiesced and ended the call.

"Why do I feel like this is the dumbest idea we've had since going to that club without telling the guys?" Jen asked as she stood.

"How were we supposed to know they'd flip their lids over a little dancing?" Sally asked.

"Let's just get this over with," future Jacque told them as she headed for the door.

Chapter 11

Jacque blinked several times to clear her head after the Great Luna once again moved them through time and space. She looked around to get her bearings, expecting to be with Jen, Sally, and her future self. Instead she was faced with the males of the Romania pack all stuffed into a large SUV. It was a lot of dominance squished into a small enclosed space.

"Why did I wait to come?" Fane snarled. "I told you I wasn't going to like what I found," he said shooting his Alpha a glare.

"You can't dwell on what could have been," Vasile told him. "You are here now and you know without a doubt that she is yours." He turned then and looked at Decebel. "Why are you challenging for the blonde female?"

Jacque's heart broke all over for Decebel as she saw him wrestling with the emotions he didn't understand because, just like the first time, there were no mating signs between him and Jen.

"Honestly, Alpha, I don't know. I saw that mutt touching her and my wolf nearly took over. I've never responded to any female that way. But I can't get into her mind. There's a connection, but I don't understand it."

Vasile stared thoughtfully at his Beta. "I'm sure there is an explanation for it. What happens when you win the challenge? Will you leave her here?"

Decebel growled. "Until I understand what's happening, where she is, I will be."

"That's what I was afraid of," Vasile muttered.

"I don't know what you guys are fretting about," Costin spoke up from the back of the vehicle. "We've found our true mates *and* we get to wipe the floor with some cocky wolves that need to be put in their place. How is this not a win-win?"

Sorin clapped him on the back as he shook his head. "The glass is always half full to you isn't it?"

Costin shrugged. "Would you rather be like those two who both look like they've found a pit of vipers instead of their true mates?"

To Jacque's surprise, Fane turned around so fast that she felt the breeze of his movement on her face. His glowing blue eyes and inhumanly long teeth had made an appearance as he narrowed his eyes on Costin. "Of course, I'm thankful I've found my true mate. But forgive me if it's a little disturbing to find her in the arms of another wolf," Fane snarled. His posture seemed to deflate as he sat back down. "I've already seen too much," he said, more to himself than the others. "Jacquelyn doesn't know to block her thoughts or memories and they've been together for two years. I don't blame her. She knows that she is half Canis lupus, but she didn't know about true mates. What I don't understand is why her mother didn't tell her about them."

"We don't know everything, son," Vasile said. "I understand how hard it is to see your mate with another male, but until you know everything, you need to save your questions."

"You've seen her thoughts about their physical relationship?" Decebel asked.

Jacque saw the glint of violence in his eyes. It was something she'd seen before and something she never wanted to be on the receiving end of.

Fane's jaw clenched as he gave a rigid single nod.

"You can at least be glad he is a wolf. If he was human, you wouldn't be allowed to rip the arms that held your mate from his body."

"Or gouge out the eyes that have seen what only you should be allowed to see," Costin added a little too eagerly.

"Holy crap, they're a blood thirsty group," future Jacque whispered.

"You know how strong their protective instincts are. I am actually surprised they have had this much self-control, especially Decebel. The darkness is heavy in him. He has been too long without his true mate at this point."

"We are not animals!" Vasile snarled at the males. "We do not lose control and act like ravenous beasts because of jealousy!"

Jacque was shocked when Fane growled at his father. "That is exactly what we are!" He smacked his chest with the flat of his palm. "I have a beast inside of me and he is a part of me. A part of me is an animal. Do not expect me to act like a man! He knew the rules. Jacquelyn maybe innocent in this, but Lucas Steele is not. He knew when no mating signs appeared that she wasn't his, which meant she belonged to someone else, and he touched her anyway. He will be lucky if I don't rip him apart piece by offending piece."

Jacque noticed that Decebel's breathing had increased with every word Fane spoke. The Beta obviously wasn't unaffected by the description Fane was sharing so eloquently. Jacque herself was surprised by her mate's anger. The first time she'd met Fane he had been so calm and in control. The man before her was more like the wolf; she gasped as the realization hit her.

"He's dealing with exactly the same thing that he experienced in the In-Between," she said to the Great Luna as she rubbed her forehead. "Bloody freaking hell! It wouldn't matter what I did, he would still face the same thing."

"But in this instance, he is dealing with reality, not some horrible trick of the In-Between. The things he has witnessed through this Jacque's memories really happened."

"Oh shit, please tell me I didn't sleep with Lucas." Jacque's stomach churned dangerously as she thought about Fane having to see something like that in her mind.

"Not in the way that you mean," the goddess reassured. Though, truly, it didn't give her any relief. Even if Fane witnessed Lucas embracing her, that would be painful enough.

Her attention was drawn back to the males when Vasile pushed his power throughout the vehicle and had every man lowering their heads unable to move.

"I am your Alpha and you will obey me. The challenge is to the death. That is your recompense for the offense of him touching your mate. You will not be overly brutal in taking his life."

"No disrespect, Alpha," Decebel spoke but it sounded strained and painful. Jacque was surprised he could even do that much, but then she remembered that Decebel was an Alpha in his own right. He submitted to Vasile because he had not wanted to be an Alpha at one time. "It will take more than your command to keep me from destroying the male who had his hand on Jennifer. There are no mating signs, but my wolf recognizes her as his. No one touches what is mine, especially a male who knew better. He forfeited a dignifying death when he disrespected my female and me. Why should I show him any mercy?"

The males raised their heads slowly as Vasile pulled his power back under control. He met Decebel's glowing amber eyes and Jacque saw in his face the compassion that her father-in-law was known for. "You, above all, deserve to finally have your mate. I know that and I understand how desperately you need her. Don't let finding her turn you into what you fight so hard not to become. I concede that we have an animal, a beast, living inside of us, but the Great Luna also gave us the spirit of a man. We have the ability to reason, to think beyond the immediate moment. We have been entrusted with all of the strengths of the wolf and that of man as well. We cannot abuse that power. These wolves showed no self-control by attempting to take females that were not their true mates. Do not lower yourself to their standards by giving up your own self-control."

"I can make you no promises," Decebel admitted coolly.

The silence in the SUV was so tangible that Jacque was sure if she made a sound they would be able to hear her. Her mind was drawn back to the reasons she'd thought it would be best for Fane to have never met her and she realized how foolish she'd been.

Fane was her mate. He held the other half of her soul and she'd stupidly believed they wouldn't have found one another regardless of how long it took. They were as inevitable as the rising of the sun.

She looked over at the future Fane. He was hurting, just as the Fane in her reality was hurting. The pain that she thought to save him from had still occurred.

He lowered his head and pressed his fingertips against his forehead. His shoulders were tight and she wanted so badly to reach out and rub the stress from him.

"I just need her with me," Fane whispered into the silence. "I can handle anything as long as she is by my side."

Decebel and Costin both nodded their heads, the looks on their faces making it clear that they completely agreed with his statement.

Decebel's head snapped around to look out of the window and Jacque followed the direction of his stare. That was when she realized they were just down the street from her house. A small smile appeared on her face; she should have known they wouldn't have been far.

"What the hell are they doing now?" Decebel growled as they watched the three girls step out of her front door.

The males waited until they were several houses away before they climbed silently from the vehicle and started to follow them. Jacque and the Great Luna were suddenly out of the SUV, without having to lift a leg, and walking with the males. They'd only gone about twenty feet when Vasile motioned for them to stop.

All of the males lifted their noses into the air and breathed. Snarls followed as they confirmed what Jacque already knew.

"Lucas and some of his pack are here," Vasile said, speaking so softly that only werewolf hearing would pick it up.

Decebel started to continue forward but Vasile stopped him. "They will catch our scent as well if the direction of the wind changes." He turned to Fane and Costin. "Can either of you track your mates through the mental bond?"

Fane nodded. "She doesn't realize it, but I have complete access to her mind."

"Not like he would have stayed out anyway," Jacque muttered.

"Then we will follow them." Vasile motioned for them to get back in the vehicle.

"We're just going to let the girls go with those mongrels?" Decebel asked incredulously.

"A wise man not only picks his battles carefully but also his battlefield," Vasile said, placing a hand on his Beta's shoulder. "Trust me."

After several tense heartbeats, Decebel nodded and loaded up with the others.

The Great Luna placed a hand on Jacque and they too were once again in the SUV with the males.

"Why would Lucas break the rules of the challenge?" Fane asked as his leg bounced restlessly. "He knows now that we don't have to wait. We can attack immediately and it won't be just the three we challenged."

"Heck yeah!" Costin hollered. "A good brawl is just what we need. Well, really what we need is our females, but I don't think they're just going to jump in our arms and let us have our way with them, so a brawl is the next best thing."

Jacque laughed as the others looked at Costin as though he'd lost his mind. Of all the males, Costin had always been the most laid back, but she'd seen that laid back did not mean submissive. Costin would hold his own with the best of them. His pretty smile and flirty ways only hid the aggressive, possessive wolf beneath.

Fane gave directions to Vasile as he searched through future Jacque's mind. Every now and then he'd let out a muttered curse and Jacque knew she didn't want to know what it was that was causing that reaction in him.

"Are you going to make me watch this?" Jacque asked the Great Luna. "I've seen my mate in so many battles, but judging by his mind set right now, I don't know if I want to watch him fight."

The Great Luna looked back at her and Jacque knew she saw everything. There was no hiding her fears, her joys, her sadness, or pain. The goddess saw it all and Jacque hoped she'd have mercy on her.

Jacque felt her hand once again on her arm and again came the pulling sensation. She opened her eyes and saw that they were in the woods, but she knew instantly it wasn't Romania. She heard the snarls and growls and turned to see a flurry of claws and fangs. So, she wasn't going to be spared the violence after all.

"I have my reasons," the Great Luna said as she moved closer to where the males fought. They were in various forms, some in their human bodies and some in their wolf. Jacque recognized Fane in his black wolf form with crystal blue eyes as he circled his prey.

It all seemed too familiar, except this time Decebel, Sorin, Costin, and Vasile were fighting as well. It was by no means a fair fight. Several of Lucas' pack members had joined in and were double-teaming some of the Romania pack males, but they still weren't as powerful and Decebel and Vasile who picked them off like flies.

Jacque heard her own scream and looked up to see her future self surrounded by Jen and Sally as they each watched in horror. The guys they'd been dating were fighting for their lives, and losing. Jacque blinked and suddenly she wasn't looking out of her own eyes anymore. She was seeing out of future Jacque's eyes and feeling her emotions. She felt her best friend's hands in her own and heard her own heartbeat pounding like a drum in her chest.

She watched Fane fight and realized that though future Jacque didn't know him, she couldn't stand to bear the thought of him hurt. She was upset with herself for not being worried about Lucas, but she couldn't deny her connection with Fane. So much confusion warred inside of her as they watched Fane lunge forward and grab Lucas by the neck and shake him like a rag doll. He released the wolf and jumped back out of the reach of Lucas' sharp teeth. They danced back and forth like that for a few moments with Fane scoring a bite here and there. Jacque realized that Fane was just toying with Lucas. And her future self realized it as well.

"Finish it all ready. You aren't a damn cat to play with your food. Can you not let him live?" Somehow Jacque heard the thought that future Jacque sent to Fane.

"I realize you do not understand everything because this fool kept you ignorant, and I'm sorry that it will hurt you to see him die, but I cannot break the rules of the challenge. He knew you were not his mate and yet he claimed you anyway. In our world, that is forfeiting one's life." Fane continued to fight with Lucas as he spoke to her but she noticed that he was no longer playing. He attacked with a ferocity that future Jacque had never seen and didn't understand. In less than a minute from the time she told him to finish him, Fane had Lucas by the neck as his body hung at an odd angle.

Fane looked up and met future Jacque's eyes, and Jacque felt all of his turmoil. *"This is not how I wanted us to meet. I should have come to you sooner. I should have been here to protect you and bring you into our world gently, not with death and anger. I am sorry, Luna."*

Jacque had been trying to spare him these types of feelings. Now, as she stood there seeing Fane from inside her future self, she realized there was no such thing as sparing someone pain.

Chapter 12

"I'm not leaving this forest until I know she's alright," Jen snapped as she awkwardly limped through the dark woods on her one-shoed feet. Decebel was steadily grumbling behind her.

"I think you've helped enough for one night, Jennifer," he growled.

"I don't know what you're so bent out of shape about," she said swinging around to glare at him. "I kept all my clothes on."

He raised a brow at her as he pointedly looked at the foot that was missing a shoe.

Jen rolled her eyes. "Oh, give me a damn break. You're the only guy I know who thinks feet are sexy. It's not my fault you have some jacked up fetish that makes you get all growly when I take off my shoes."

Decebel crossed his arms in front of his chest as he looked down at her. He was even more handsome now than he'd been when they met. Maybe it was because she knew him better, or maybe it had something to do with bringing a life into the world together.

Whatever the reason, it only pissed her off more when she was attempting to be mad at him and he had to go and look sexy.

"Stupid, yummy werewolves," she huffed as she met his glare.

"Why did you come after her without telling me what your plan was? Why did you shut me out?" The second question was bit out as his jaw clenched. "We are a team, Jennifer. Where you go, I go. How can we be a team if you won't be honest with me?"

"I never lied to you," Jen pointed out. "Not really."

"Twisting the truth so that it isn't technically a lie does not make it right," he parried.

"Maybe not in your land but in Jennifer-ville where I am the mayor, it's totally acceptable behavior."

His head dropped back as a frustrated sigh blew out of him. Jen actually felt sorry for him. Being mated to her was really more of a form of punishment most days. She wondered if he ever thought about what he could have possibly done to deserve such a fate.

"You try my patience, but you are not a form of punishment," he said in a much gentler voice than his face conveyed.

Jen had opened the bond back up completely, and even though she'd been the one to partially close it, it was a relief to have the intimacy and rightness of it back in place.

"It's not that I don't want to tell you things, B, it's just that I know you'd tie me to the bed and not let me out of your sight if you knew some of the things I want to do."

"There are many nights that you don't complain about such things." His voice was low as his eyes narrowed on her.

She held up a hand. "Talking dirty to me is not going to distract me." She paused. "Okay, so my tract record with that isn't exactly stellar. It's not going to work this time." She took a step toward him wanting to touch him but knowing that would only lead to things that needed to wait. "I knew that if I told you I didn't have a clue where Jacque was and I was walking around in the mountains at night, you would blow a gasket."

His scowl deepened, if that were even possible. "And rightfully so! You're my mate, the mother of my pup, and I've only had to watch you die a couple of times in the past year. Why on earth would I possibly not want you roaming through the forest after dark—especially one known for harboring practitioners of dark magic?"

"Sarcasm really doesn't suit you," Jen told him, placing her hands on her hips.

"When are you going to realize that I can't change my nature? I will forever be too protective of you, unreasonably possessive of you, hyper vigilante of my duty to guard you, and constantly unable to quench my need to put you in a plastic bubble?" Decebel rubbed a hand across his jaw as Jen stared at his chiseled face.

"I get that it's in your nature to be those things, Dec, but that doesn't change the fact that I am always going to be independent and feel the need to protect those I love, with or without your approval."

They stared at each other for several minutes before he finally looked away. He didn't look down; he wasn't about to show submissive behavior. "I suppose we are at an impasse."

Jen shrugged. "Wouldn't be the first time and sure as heck won't be the last." Jen scanned the forest around her yet again hoping to see signs of Fane and Jacque making their way through it, but just like the fifteen other times she'd done it, the only movement was the wind rippling through the leaves and brush.

"If Fane doesn't whip the snot out of her for taking off like this, you can bet that I'm going to," Jen growled as she found a comfortable spot against a large tree trunk. She patted the ground next to her and smiled up at her still irritated mate. "Pretend we're on a romantic date," she told him.

Decebel snorted but sat down next to her. "A romantic date in the dark, cold, freaky mountains?"

Jen smacked his leg. "Don't be cute. That's my job."

Decebel wrapped an arm around her and pulled Jen tight against his side. She snuggled in and buried her face against his chest, breathing in deep and enjoying the scent of her man. There were few things she enjoyed more than the way Decebel smelled.

"Good to know," he murmured having heard her train of thought.

They sat in companionable silence for several minutes before Jen let out a sigh. "If someone told you a year and a half ago that you'd be sitting on the ground in the mountains of Romania with your mate, whom you'd just recently had a child with, what would you have said?" she asked him. She felt his hand slide up her arm and back down again, attempting to rub some heat into her.

"I probably would have told them to give me some of what they were smoking," he admitted.

Jen laughed. "Whatever. You wouldn't have said something so chill. You didn't start talking like a normal person until you met me."

"There are lots of things I didn't do until I met you," Decebel said gently as his hand traveled back up her arm, past her shoulder to her neck, where it rested possessively.

"Back at ya," Jen said as she patted his flat stomach. She paused and then added, "What do you think you'd be doing right now if we hadn't met?"

"I don't like to think about my life without you."

"Was it really that bad?"

Decebel let out a long sigh. "I sometimes forget that you really haven't been a part of this life for very long. Because of that, you don't fully realize the darkness that is in the males until we meet our true mates."

Jen pulled back to look up at him. He was right. She didn't fully understand it but then how could she? She was a middle class, American girl from a semi-normal family. Jen had never had to experience two centuries of growing emptiness while a beast inside slowly takes over.

"But if someone had told me this is where I'd be in a year and a half, I definitely wouldn't have believed them." Decebel's hand massaged Jen's neck causing a shiver to run through her that had nothing to do with the cold mountain air. "I had given up hope on finding a mate and part of me really didn't want one."

Jen held up a hand. "Stop. Go no further. I completely remember you not wanting a mate because you were worried you wouldn't be able to protect her. Good thing for you, I didn't really care what your worries were because all I knew was that you were mine."

Decebel's hand tightened on her neck and tilted her head back. With his other hand he ran his fingertip across her lips, over her chin, and down her neck. Jen was frozen, helpless, and utterly mesmerized by her mate's glowing eyes and firm touch. He whispered something to her in Romanian and she felt her cheeks flush. Decebel leaned closer to her until his lips were nearly touching hers. "I have always been yours," he whispered against her mouth. "Just as you have always been mine and will always be mine."

"And you still want me even when I'm—" She couldn't finish because Decebel had pressed his lips against hers. Jen was amazed that every kiss still made her stomach drop to her toes and her palms sweat. There was a time when she thought that those feelings would fade, that she would grow used to his touch, but she'd been wrong. Every fingertip across her skin, every trail of his lips down her neck, and every breath mingled with her own only increased her attraction to him. As his hand wrapped itself in her hair, holding her still as he kissed her greedily, Jen pressed against him. She growled, unable to get close enough to her mate to satisfy the growing need.

Decebel continued to ravish her mouth even as he used their bond to speak to her. *"I still want you. Nothing will ever change that. If you keep up that line of thinking, I will cease being a gentleman and will simply take what I want."*

Jen smiled against his lips. *"How many times do I have to tell you that you can't take what is freely offered."*

"Are you offering yourself, Jennifer?" His voice was rough with need as he pulled her tighter against him.

"No, I think I like this whole idea of you taking what you want. So, consider this my response to your forwardness. Dec, we have to stop. No, I won't be seduced. Stop, you animal." Jen's voice was dry as she reached to him through their bond. She could feel his humor but his desire for her was quickly dowsing all other emotions.

Decebel's breaths were coming in shallow gasps as he pulled back from the kiss. Jen didn't know when he had pushed her onto her back but there she was with her mate hovering breathlessly over her. His eyes glowed bright amber and she smiled up at him. "Hello, wolf," she teased knowing that his beast was every bit as present as the man was.

"Mine," he growled back at her.

Jen's smile widened. If Decebel had been reduced to single word responses, then there would be no stopping him—not that she had any intention of that. So, Jen did what she does best, she poked the already agitated wolf. She leaned up, closing the small space he'd put between them. Her lips were a hair's breadth away from his as she spoke. "Prove it."

Chapter 13

Fane's paws padded angrily against the ground as he moved through the forest. She wasn't here. He knew it with every fiber of his being and yet, because it was the last place she'd been, he couldn't bring himself to leave. The Great Luna had said that Jacquelyn was safe, but Fane needed to see her and touch her to truly believe that. His wolf was a snarling mess as he tried to figure out what he could do to get their mate back, and when he kept coming up empty, he snarled even more.

He wandered the forest pathways aimlessly. Fane came around a large boulder and stopped short as he felt magic roll over his fur. He froze, letting only his eyes move over the area surrounding him. Something had changed. He'd felt it as surely as if he'd walked from an air conditioned building out into the summer heat. Fane didn't see anyone but all his surroundings had changed. He could tell that he wasn't in the same forest he'd been in only seconds before.

Finally, he took several steps forward, all of his senses on high alert, probing for any threat. As he slowly turned in a circle taking in the changes in scenery, a power stronger than he'd ever felt before forced him to his knees.

His head bowed low and his fur receded, replaced by his human flesh. Fane took several shaky breathes. He hadn't forced the change and no one in his realm, not even his Alpha, could have pushed his phase back as simply and as easily. He knew that it wouldn't do him any good to try and retaliate against the offender. No beings but the Fates and the Great Luna had such power. And this wasn't the Great Luna. The Fates didn't visit mortals, even supernatural wolves such as him, on a whim. As such, Fane wasn't about to do anything rash. He stood, his legs still wobbly, and raised his head to look at the three beings before him. They stood there pulsating from form to form—sometimes appearing as a human, sometimes as an animal, and sometimes as something else entirely.

A pair of plain, black pants, definitely not manmade, appeared in front of him. He reached for them and slipped them on, never taking his eyes off the pulsating forms before him.

"Fane Lupei, son of the Romania pack Alpha, prince to his kind, mate of Jacquelyn Lupei, soon to be father of your own heir." The combined voices of the Fates filled the area around Fane as though surround sound speakers had been installed in the forest. As he stared at the beings that pulsated before him, he shuddered at having their undivided attention fully focused on him and naming him so thoroughly.

He bowed his head once to acknowledge them, but he didn't ask them what they wanted. If the Fates had shown themselves to him, there was a reason and they would get around to it when they were good and ready.

"Your mate has requested an audience with us."

Apparently they were good and ready then. His breath caught in his throat and it felt as if a sack of concrete had fallen into his stomach. Jacquelyn wanted to see the Fates? Why didn't she tell him? Was she in some sort of danger or trouble? The questions began to pile up faster than he could begin to come up with plausible answers.

"She wishes to make it so that you had not met," they began but as soon as the words hit his ears Fane couldn't hear anything else.

Blood filled his ears as the beating of his heart increased to a speed and intensity that was painful. His mate was trying to change their fate. He felt as though a knife had been stabbed repeatedly into his heart and lungs and he couldn't catch his breath. He knew Jacquelyn loved him, he could feel the intensity of that love when their bond was open, but it didn't take away the feelings of betrayal and doubt. Whatever twisted reason she had for wanting to do something so desperate, it wasn't because she didn't want him or love him. Regardless, he was pissed.

"Have you granted her request?" Fane finally managed to ask the Fates still pulsating before him.

"We have not met with her. We were intrigued by such a request, but when we approached her, she had been taken by the Great Luna. We can only assume that the goddess is attempting to explain the consequences of such a request."

"At least someone is trying to talk some sense into her," Fane growled under his breath.

"Step forward, Fane Lupei, and we will show you what your mate is seeing so that you too will understand the ramifications of her wishes."

"Please, Fates, hear me now. I beg of you. Do not grant her this," Fane pleaded. He was prepared to drop to his knees and grovel if it was necessary. His foolish, foolish mate, what had she done?

"Come, mortal," the voices said in unison.

Fane took a shaky hesitant step toward the Fates. He was apprehensive about what he would see, but there was also a sick curiosity like turning your head to stare at a terrible automobile accident on the highway. Suddenly, he felt a warmth rush over him as his knees again hit the ground and everything around him went dark.

Images began to play in his mind as he watched himself make the decision not to follow his wolf's instincts and go to Coldspring. He wanted to roar at himself, cursing inwardly, at his inability to move or speak as he watched a nightmare unfold before him: Jacquelyn meeting Lucas Steele, going on dates with him, kissing him, and looking at him with adoration in her eyes. Fane did, however, note that there was no love in her eyes, at least not the love that she looked at him with. He watched her relationship with Lucas rip apart her friendships and then, to his surprise, he watched Jen and Sally find relationships with other wolves in the Coldspring pack. It was all wrong—so very, very wrong. Surely if this is what she was seeing with the Great Luna then she was seeing that this was not what was best. How could it be? When he got glimpses of himself he watched the darkness grow inside of him as his beast raged against the man. His wolf knew that their mate was not in Romania and still Fane refused to listen.

It was his father who finally forced the issue. As Fane watched that version of his and Jacquelyn's story unfold, he saw that their meeting was as set as the sun rise. They were meant for each other and no matter how she attempted to change it, they would end up together. Fane realized then that there were some fates that were unavoidable. The only variable was how difficult the people involved decided to make the journey. In the reality that played like a movie in his mind, there was so much more pain and hurt because of the path they had taken to find one another. Fane had to endure seeing his mate standing beside another male, one that believed he had the right to touch her and kiss her when she in fact belonged with Fane.

He still had to fight for her, but because Lucas was more attached to her, not to mention Sally and Jen's attached wolves, this battle was much bloodier. So many more wolves lost their lives as Fane watched the two packs tear into each other.

This was the future that could happen if the Fates granted his mate's request. "Not in my bloody lifetime," Fane vowed as he continued to live out the battle for his mate. As soon as the vision faded, Fane slumped forward onto his hands. His breathing was fast and shallow as if he had actually been in the fight. His muscles shook with exertion though he hadn't actually been doing anything, and sweat ran down his back despite the cold temperature.

"Are you going to grant her request?" Fane asked through the shallow gasps. When there was no answer he slowly raised his head to find he was alone. "Figures," he muttered. "Stick around long enough to dig in the knife but don't bother to remove it."

After several more minutes of attempting to re-gather his senses, Fane sat back on his haunches. He reached up with both hands and ran his fingers through his hair, pulling just a little, hoping the pain would clear the rest of his muddled thoughts. He had to get to Jacquelyn. He couldn't let this happen. No matter what good she thought it could possibly do, it would cause more harm. It wouldn't just affect their lives. Like a line of dominos falling as the first one was pushed, the lives of those around them would come crashing down. He truly understood the full meaning of the saying the path to hell was paved with good intentions.

"*JACQUELYN!*" Fane thundered through their bond. He pushed with all of his power, even drawing on his father's power, which was something he rarely did. He was desperate. More than ever Fane needed his mate to understand just how important their destiny with each other was.

He couldn't do that if he couldn't talk to her, see her, or touch her.

His chest restricted even tighter when he finally felt her. She was scared, devastated, and full of guilt. She wouldn't answer him which only served to enrage his wolf.

"You cannot do this, Luna! This is not a decision you get to make for us. ANSWER ME." Fane knew he probably looked like a mad man kneeling on the forest floor with his teeth elongated and claws stretch from his fingertips. He was barely holding it together. The sound of her voice in his mind was his undoing.

"I only wanted to take away your pain. Is that so wrong?"

Chapter 14

Jacque squeezed her eyes closed so tightly it was almost painful. She couldn't get the images out of her mind. So much blood and death, so much pain and confusion, because they hadn't met as they should have when she was still in high school—before she'd shared her emotions with another and before Fane and his father's wolves had needed to kill half a pack.

Fane's anger was like a tidal wave rushing through her as he suddenly shoved himself into her mind. The bond wasn't fully open but it was enough that she could hear him and he was beyond enraged. She didn't know how he'd found out what she'd done, and her heart ached to feel how much it hurt him. His voice boomed in her mind but she couldn't respond, at least not right away. She had to gather her emotions to regain some semblance of control.

"Your mate is quite upset," the Great Luna's voice broke through her carefully crafted bubble of silence.

Jacque opened her eyes to find them back in the small clearing where the large boulder rested with her things sitting on top of it. Her stomach dropped as she looked at the bowl with her blood in it. Why had she thought that was a good idea? Fane's emotions were all over the place, making it hard for her to think. She knew she needed to respond to him, but she was too ashamed.

"ANSWER ME." His words echoed in her mind and Jacque felt her heart break for the anguish he was feeling. When he was already dealing with so much, she had added to his struggles.

"I only wanted to take away your pain. Is that so wrong?" she finally whispered again, this time allowing him to hear her thoughts. A sob caught in her throat. She was crying more out of anger than sadness—anger at herself for being so stupid, anger at the world for being so hard, anger at everything—because it was easier to be angry than to think about how she'd hurt her mate now that he'd found out her plan.

"Just talk to him, Jacquelyn," the Great Luna told her. "You know now, that though your heart was in the right place, your actions would not have yielded the best outcome."

"What if you hadn't intervened?" Jacque asked through clenched teeth as tears tracked down her cheeks. "What if I'd been able to go through with it?"

"Then it would have been a tough lesson."

Jacque let out a derisive snort. "Like this isn't?" Her head dropped down so low that her chin nearly touched her chest. She felt defeated.

The Great Luna's hand gently ran down Jacque's head. "It is a tough lesson, yes. But the direst consequences have been avoided. It is a gift. Take it and learn from it and move forward. Yes, you must now deal with the possessive wrath of your mate, but know that he is only angry because he loves you so much. You will get through this and you will come out stronger on the other side."

Jacque knew the minute she was alone. The warmth that seemed to follow the Great Luna was suddenly gone and she was once again on her own, alone in the cold.

"Where are you?" Fane asked and though he sounded a little calmer, Jacque wasn't fooled.

Three voices filled the clearing before she could answer him.

"Do you still wish to petition us for your request?"

Jacque whipped around to see the forms of the Fates about ten feet away from her. No longer was she in the same part of the forest as she had just been standing. Her eyes widened briefly as she'd forgotten that they might actually answer her.

She shook her head. "N-n-no," she stuttered out. "I take it back. I don't want to change anything."

"You have seen what could be?"

"Yes."

"You know now that you should not attempt to alter what has been put in place?"

"Yes." Jacque didn't know what else to say. She wanted to scream 'I got it,' but decided not to push her luck.

"Then it is time you were reunited with your mate and you finish what destiny has started." The forms faded from view and the forest around her seemed to morph before her eyes, bringing her back to a familiar landscape. She turned in a slow circle as she began to recognize that she was once again in the forest beyond the mansion. She heard a low growl from behind her and she squeezed her eyes closed.

"I know you're angry."

Fane chuckled deep and low and Jacque felt her stomach drop.

"You have no idea, Luna."

She turned slowly to face him. Her hand instinctively landing on her stomach as his eyes dropped to her abdomen.

"Are you alright?" he asked carefully.

She nodded.

"Is my child alright?"

She nodded again.

Fane let out a slow breath before finally speaking again. "We will return home. Then we will discuss what has happened. You must be cold and hungry and I will see to your needs before we deal with this any further."

As much as those things were true, Jacque would almost rather just get it done. It was like when she was a child and her mother would tell her that when they got home she would be getting a spanking. The anticipation was worse than the actual spanking ever could have been.

"I can't do this now, Jacquelyn. I am too upset," Fane admitted having picked up on her thoughts. She realized that the bond was fully open and he was not attempting to mask his presence in her mind. As her mate, he had every right to be in her mind—just like he had every right to her body and her time and her affection and anything else. She was his and yet just as he had done to her, she'd withheld a part of herself from him. When would they ever learn?

Fane reached out his hand to her and she took it allowing the warmth from him to reach deep inside of her and relieve the ache that had been building. Being separated from him sucked and yet she'd done it willingly.

"Do you hear that?" Jen asked as she lay wrapped in Decebel's arms. They were leaning back against a large tree trunk, and she wasn't about to wipe away the goofy grin that had been spread across her face since her mate had begun his pursuit of her. So she'd been a little easy and let him conquer her without a fight; her mate could be quite persuasive when he put his mind to it.

"Footsteps," Decebel confirmed. He stood up and pulled Jen to her feet. She brushed herself off and turned to face the direction of the noise. A few minutes later, a very ticked off looking Fane and forlorn looking Jacque emerged from the trees.

Jen ran to Jacque and threw her arms around her. She squeezed tight and pressed her mouth close to her ear. "I won't rip you a new one right now because you look as though you're kicking yourself enough for the both of us. But if you ever take off like that again, all bets are off."

Jacque nodded but didn't say anything.

Jen pulled away and took a second look at her friend. Whatever it was that she'd been up to, it had put her through the ringer and caused her mate to flip his ever loving lid.

"Jennifer, perhaps, we should go on ahead. We need to get back and see to Thia," Decebel said gently as he reached out a hand for her. Jen gave Jacque one last look before taking Decebel's hand and letting him lead her away. She didn't want to go. She wanted to know what had happened and what had put that defeated look in her friend's eyes. But Jacque was Fane's wife and some things weren't her business anymore. Jen didn't like it, but she understood. She just hoped that Jacque would be willing to open up to her later. She loved the redhead like a sister and wanted to help in any way she could, even if it was only as a shoulder to lean on.

"They will be fine," Decebel said silently to her. Her anxiety was rolling off of her and through their bond.

"Fane looked like a rabid dog. Whatever it is, it's not something that a simply apology is going to fix," Jen pointed out.

"Perhaps not, but we mate for life. They have nothing but time to work it out."

Jen squeezed his hand as she looked up at him. *"Is that why you sometimes just shake your head and walk away from a fight, which you know I hate by the way."*

Decebel chuckled. *"Baby, you know there's almost nothing I like better than a good fight with you. But there are just some things that don't deserve our emotional energy. Why waste it on trivial things? If I walk away, then you have to think about the situation rationally. And you come to that realization much quicker than if I tried to convince you of it."*

"Stupid, smart werewolf," she growled.

"Stupid, smart?"

"Shut up, you know what I mean."

"I'll take your backhanded comment simply because I know that as long as I'm on the receiving

end of your torment, it means you love me. It's when you ignore me that I know I should be worried."

"*See?*" Jen smiled up at him. "*You're stupid smart.*"

Decebel released her hand and smacked her on her backside. "Behave."

"And bore you to tears? No thank you."

Chapter 15

As Jacque and Fane made their way down the hall to their room, her stomach began to churn. She knew she had to face Fane. They needed to talk, to open up about their fears and worries, but Jacque felt so raw. It was as if all of her flesh had been removed, leaving her nerve endings exposed to the elements around her.

Jacque could feel the anger radiating off of Fane, and for the first time in a while, it wasn't him she wanted to run to. There's a saying, *sometimes only a mother will do*, and that's how Jacque suddenly felt in that moment. She was six months pregnant with her first child, she was emotional and had made a stupid impulsive decision, and—by golly—she just wanted her mama.

Fane opened the door and stepped aside so that she could enter before him. Jacque's heart felt as though it was going to beat straight up her throat and out of her mouth. She swallowed hard as she turned to face Fane. He closed the door quietly behind him.

His movements were slow and calculated like a coil being turned tighter and tighter.

They stood there facing each other, Jacque watching him while Fane's eyes were fixed on the floor. She noticed his hands clenching and unclenching. She wanted to say something, but her brain was flooded with emotions, and words would not form into any coherent thought.

After several minutes of tense silence, Fane's voice caused her to shiver.

"What do you need?"

Jacque's brow drew together as she looked at him. "What?" She wasn't being obtuse; she just didn't understand what he was asking.

"Right now," Fane said slowly. "What do you need right now, in this moment?"

For you to not be so patient and understanding. A voice inside of her answered though she didn't say that out loud. "I," she started but then stopped because how do you tell your mate that you need your mama?

"Jacquelyn, I have told you from the beginning that your needs would always come first. Regardless of the fact that I want to know why you were doing what you were,

I need to make sure you are taken care of. We can deal with the rest after."

Jacque felt tears building in her eyes which only served to frustrate her more. She felt like a child. When she still didn't say anything, Fane reached into the bag he'd carried for her and pulled out her cell phone. He dialed a number and met her eyes as he waited for whoever it was he was calling to answer. She could have looked through their bond into his thoughts, but she didn't want to hear anything that would reveal just how truly angry and disappointed with her that he was.

"Lilly."

Jacque's head snapped up at the sound of her mother's name on Fane's lips.

"Well, I don't know if it's necessarily fine but she isn't in danger or hurt. But. . ." Fane paused as his blue eyes met Jacque's. "I think my mate needs to spend some time with you."

Jacque tuned out the rest of the conversation. She was too taken aback that Fane had called her mom. She had thought she'd been hiding at least those emotions from him, but they must have been flowing off of her like rain off a slanted roof.

Several minutes later, Jacque looked up when she felt a hand under her chin. She would know that touch anywhere and she welcomed it. Her eyes met Fane's. She wanted to say she was sorry and wanted to explain that she wasn't trying to avoid him.

"I love you," he told her, his deep voice soothing her. "This isn't over and I am angry with you, but that doesn't change the fact that I choose to love you no matter what. We'll talk about everything once you've spent some time with your mom. She's already on her way." He leaned forward quickly and pressed a kiss to her lips. It was firm, commanding her attention, and yet it was also a promise of his words. Fane loved her, no matter what. He. Loved. Her.

"You know that I love you right? And I'm here for you?" Lilly told her daughter as they sat in the indoor garden of the Romania Pack mansion. It was still one of Jacque's favorite places to go when she needed to think or decompress. It was a two-hour drive— capable by only the most rugged four wheel drive vehicles—down windy mountain roads across rocky terrain from Cypher's mountain to the mansion. Lilly had made it in an hour and a half.

Jacque nodded. "How are things with Cypher?" she asked, clearly stalling. The look her mother gave her made it clear that the older woman was aware of her tactics. Luckily she played along.

"It's interesting." Lilly smiled and the light in her eyes made Jacque feel a tiny bit better. She was so thankful that her mom had found someone. Regardless of whether she'd ever said it, she'd pined for Dillon. Even though she knew that he would never be hers again, she had loved him for all those years.

"I imagine living with warlocks would definitely be interesting." Jacque grinned though she could tell it didn't reach her eyes.

Lilly stared back at her, waiting patiently, making it clear that she was going to let Jacque open up at her own pace.

Might as well go ahead get this band-aid ripped off, Jacque thought to herself. Once the flood gates opened, everything just came pouring out. Jacque told her about Fane and the nightmares, about her insecurities about being a mother, about her worries for Fane and what he was going through, and finally about how she'd made the brilliant decision to seek out help from the Fates. She told Lilly about the Great Luna coming to her and doing the whole *Ghosts of Christmas past* deal and about how awful it had been to watch her life play out without Fane in it. Once every ounce of the story had been recounted Jacque sat in silence waiting for her mother's response.

"I know that must have been very painful to see," Lilly began. "And though you know now that it wouldn't have been the right decision, it was something you needed to see. Sometimes we truly think the grass is greener when in fact all grass withers as seasons change, and then it regrows healthy and green once again. You and Fane are going to have to learn to give not only each other grace but yourselves as well." Lilly paused and her eyes took on that faraway look that said she was remembering something from a long time ago. "You also need to accept that though it sucks to make mistakes or poor choices good can come of them. You can let this experience draw you and Fane closer together; you can let it help you learn that there are different seasons in life and some are more difficult than others but they all pass. You just need to find the joy even in those difficult seasons because that is what will help you get through them intact. Right now, though you are terrified of being a mom—which is totally normal—the silver lining is that you are going to have this precious little life that you and Fane created together." A single tear ran down her mom's cheek as Lilly smiled at her. "I don't think it's possible to truly grasp what it will feel like the first time you hold your baby. It's scary, exciting, overwhelming, and unbelievably life changing all at once. When you start to feel those insecurities—which will come ever more frequently as you get closer to your due date—just take a deep breath and remember, that just like Fane was destined for you, this baby was destined for you and Fane. You are the parents that he or she needs. You are the ones who were deemed best to love, nurture, and discipline your baby. It is one of the greatest honors bestowed upon humans to create life and then sustain it. You will learn what it means to truly be selfless. You will learn what it means to love without conditions. Most of all you will learn that each day is a new day, and if we screw up on this one, we can start again tomorrow."

Jacque's hands had gravitated to her swollen abdomen on their own as her mom had spoken. She felt her child kick, moving about inside of her stomach, somehow reassuring Jacque that everything was indeed how it should be. Jacque pictured herself holding their baby for the first time and knew everything her mother said was true. She was still scared, but things seemed less daunting somehow.

"Thank you," Jacque said as she wiped her own tears away.

Lilly nodded. "That's what a mother is here for. We won't get it right a lot of the time, but occasionally we actually have profound things to say. I'm convinced we should record those moments so the rest of the time when we are stumbling around just trying to make sure we put on matching shoes every day, we can be reminded that in the midst of those times we really are getting wiser."

Jacque laughed. "Well, that at least is reassuring." Jacque let out a breath that she felt as if she'd been holding since the moment the Great Luna began their little adventure. She knew she still had to face Fane, but she did feel more grounded.

Lilly patted her leg as she stood up from their spot in the gazebo. "I'm just a phone call away if you need me, day or night."

Jacque stood and hugged Lilly. When they stepped back she saw a fleeting moment of worry on her mom's face. The hairs of the back of Jacque's neck stood on end and she was overcome with a sinking feeling. "Is everything really going okay with Cypher and the warlocks?" she asked.

Lilly started to nod but then stopped. She looked down at her fidgeting hands for a few seconds before answering. "Things between Cypher and I are good. I mean we're working through the whole over protective yet inappropriate decision of sending me away during that stuff with his brother. We are growing closer, but it is an adjustment to go from being single for eighteen years to suddenly having someone else's feelings to consider."

Jacque could tell that her mom was holding something back. "I'm not a kid anymore, Mom; you can be honest with me."

A tired smile played on Lilly's lips. "Believe me, I know you aren't a child anymore. That doesn't mean that I have lost my need to protect you. But I suppose after everything you've been through, you can handle this." She let out a deep breath before plowing forward. "Something is wrong with Cypher's people—something hard to explain. It's like. . ." She shook her head. "I mean, I don't fully understand it but it's like their magic is dying, and it's causing something inside of them to die as well."

"What kind of something?" Jacque's forehead wrinkled as her brow drew together.

Lilly seemed to be searching for the right word or words. "I don't know if you'd call it their humanity because they aren't human after all. But it's like whatever is in them that makes them rational, caring, and moral—something other than impulsive monsters— is fading away."

Jacque's mouth dropped open and then closed again. She opened it again and this time words came out. "Has Cypher told Vasile about it?"

Lilly shook her head. "You know how the different species can be. They are very protective of their own and Cypher is worried that if he lets the wolves in on what is happening then they will tell the Fae who in turn would feel the need to step in."

Jacque crossed her arms in front of her as she nodded. "I can understand that. I mean the Fae are basically the supernatural police. They are not exactly known for their diplomatic skills. The Fae are just as likely to come in guns blazing and eradicate the warlocks as to help them find a solution."

"Exactly," her mom agreed. "Cypher wants to see if he can figure it out and solve it on his own."

"Is it affecting Cypher? I mean, is he still *normal*, or well, normal for his yellow-eyed self anyway?"

Her mom laughed. "Saying Cypher is normal is like saying one of your Canis lupus males is reasonable."

As they walked through the garden to the door that led back into the mansion, Jacque touched her mom's shoulder. "You will tell us if things get worse?"

Lilly hesitated but finally nodded. "I promise."

Jacque stepped out of the garden and into the hall to find Fane leaning against the opposite wall with his arms crossed in front of his broad chest and his head bowed. Lilly walked over to him and spoke softly into his ear, so softly that Jacque couldn't make out what she was saying. Fane's shoulders tensed briefly but then relaxed. As Lilly stepped away she winked at Jacque before walking down the hall leaving Jacque and Fane alone.

Fane raised his head and Jacque took it as a good sign that his eyes had finally stopped glowing.

"Are you ready to talk to me now?" he asked gently.

Jacque bit her lip as she nodded.

Fane reached for her hand, took it, and led her back toward their room. "I need to warn you, Luna, that my wolf needs action more than words at this particular moment."

Jacque felt her pulse speed up. She knew what Fane was saying. Just like their animal cousins, the wolves craved touch—not just the intimate kind but also the reassuring kind: a pat on the shoulder, a hug, or even just a hand grazing across the back. They thrived on that touch and found comfort in it—especially during times of worry, frustration, or pain.

Jacque was pretty sure that Fane's wolf didn't just need the *reassuring* kind of touch.

"It is reassuring between mates to share themselves with one another through physical intimacy," Fane pointed out silently through their bond. She knew he wasn't going to be withdrawing from her mind anytime soon, not after she'd closed him out.

As they entered their room, Jacque turned to face Fane but that was as far as she got before her legs collapsed beneath her as a sharp pain ripped through her abdomen.

Chapter 16

Fane lunged forward as he watched his mate collapse. He caught her just before her head would have slammed into the floor.

"Jacquelyn!" Her name was a plea on his lips as he watched her face turn a ghostly shade of white. "Luna, talk to me. What's wrong?"

She didn't answer him. Instead she tried to curl in on herself as she clutched at her abdomen. With every groan that rolled out of her, Fane felt a piece of him wither away.

"Da!" Fane called out through the pack bonds. *"Something is wrong with Jacque. I think it's something with the baby."*

"I'll send Rachel. Is there any blood?" his father responded immediately.

Fane's heart plummeted; he hadn't thought about blood. He glanced down attempting to see if anything was on her jeans.

"Not that I can tell."

Fane carefully picked his mate up in his arms and carried her over to their bed.

Perspiration was gathering on her forehead as she continued to writhe in pain. She still hadn't said a coherent word but when he turned to go to the bathroom to get a towel, she grabbed his shirt. Her eyes were wide with panic. His own panic began to well up inside of him, but he fought to suppress it. He knew that he needed his wits about him right now.

"Don't leave me," she ground out between clenched teeth.

"I'm not leaving you, love. I'm not going anywhere. I just wanted to get you a towel."

She shook her head at him and clutched his shirt tighter. Fane sat down next to her, realizing that he couldn't walk away from her for any amount of time when she looked at him like that. With her large green eyes she was begging him to fix it—to take the pain away. He wanted nothing more than to do just that.

The door opened and Rachel and Gavril's scents poured in mixing with the smell of pain and fear. Fane looked up as Rachel approached on the opposite side of the bed. Her face was one of concentration and calm. She looked at him and met his stare.

"Prince, may I touch your mate?" she asked formally, reminding him that she was very, very old.

Fane nodded once but didn't back away when Rachel moved forward and placed a hand on Jacquelyn's stomach. The healer closed her eyes and Fane tried not to growl at her to hurry up. He felt a hand on his shoulder and nearly turned to snarl at whoever dared get near his mate in such a vulnerable state.

"Easy," Vasile's voice and power cascaded over him, allowing him to keep his anxious wolf from lashing out, but only just.

Rachel pushed her power into Jacque as she searched out the problem that was causing the female so much pain. The first thing that she felt was Jacque's panic and fear. She was terrified for the life of her child.

"Easy, Jacque," she whispered softly to her as she attempted to assuage some of her terror. *"I'm going to see what the problem is, and then we are going to do everything we can to make sure that you and the baby are okay."*

"Please, please, don't let my baby die."

The desperate appeal made Rachel even more determined to protect the pair. After all her years serving the packs, how many young Canis Lupus had Rachel seen born? How many small gifts had they been given? It was only a handful. She returned her energy and attention to Jacque's womb as she inspected the uterus, placenta, and then the child within. The infant's heart rate was rising. Jacque's own panic seemed to cause it to rise even further.

"Peace, little one," Rachel crooned to the child as she let her power surround the womb. It was only a few minutes later that Rachel realized the source of the pain and why the heart rate was increasing. Jacque was having contractions, and not just minor ones. These were labor contractions that, if allowed to continued, would lead to an early delivery.

"It is not time yet. You have to stay safe and warm for a little longer." Rachel attempted to

stop the contraction but all she was able to do was to lessen the intensity of it. She was surprised that she couldn't do more, but then she remembered that Jacque was half human, and it might take human medicine to help where her healing powers would not.

She kept her hand on Jacque and continued to focus on holding back the contractions as she pulled her consciousness back out. She looked at Fane and met glowing wolf eyes.

"She's in premature labor. I am able to lessen the strength of the contractions but I cannot stop them."

"What can stop them?" Vasile asked from behind his son.

Rachel glanced up at the Alpha and then back to Fane. "I think she will need human treatment of some kind."

Jacque could hear the voices around her but it was difficult to make out what they were saying. Her attention was too focused on the pain and her distress for her baby. Her hands clenched down on her stomach as another bout of pain rolled through her, though it wasn't as bad as the last one. She'd heard Rachel's voice and caught the word labor. Jacque didn't want to panic because she figured that losing control wouldn't help the situation, but at six months pregnant, she was pretty sure going into labor was not a good thing.

The sound of Jen's voice snapped her out of her internal musings. She kept her eyes closed because the one time she'd tried opening them the room had been spinning.

"Decebel, you have to wait in the hall. Crap, man, look at Fane's face. Do you really think he wants another dominant male near his pregnant mate?" Jen sounded truly exasperated, which Jacque knew was a common occurrence between the blonde and her mate.

"Now," Jen said, sounding closer than before, "would someone please like to tell me what is going on?"

Jacque listened this time as Rachel explained to Jen that she was in premature labor and would need human medicine to stop it. Once again she fought the panic that threatened to rise up and strangle her. She must have made a noise because she felt Fane's breath on her face as he whispered to her.

"I hate that you are hurting, Luna. I want to take your pain." He sounded frustrated and helpless all at the same time. "We're going to fix this; trust me to take care of you."

"Save our baby, Fane," she sent the thought to him, still struggling to keep her thoughts clear.

"I will save you both. That's my privilege and duty."

She believed him. Fane would walk through the fires of hell, *had* walked through the fires of hell for her, and he would do it as many times as he needed to in order to protect her and keep her safe. He would do the same for their child. Of that she had no doubt.

Chapter 17

Jen glanced at Jacque but couldn't offer her friend more than that. It was too hard to see her hurting like that. After all of the times they each had been in danger, after all of their close calls and by the skin of their teeth moments, Jen was gun shy. She knew that the females of their species frequently lost children—if they were able to conceive at all. But with a healer in the pack it was supposed to be less common. She had to bite her tongue to keep from snarling at Rachel and asking her why in the hell her friend was in such a situation now.

"Okay, so we get her the medicine," Jen stated matter-of-fact like. Why were they all just standing here staring at her? Why hadn't someone already gotten their asses in gear and done something? Maybe it was because she nearly lost her own child, or maybe it was because she was a mom now and she fully understood just how protective mothers were of their babies. Whatever the reason, the thought of Jacque losing her baby was beyond Jen's comprehension. It just wasn't an option, sort of like Dec being feminine or Vasile wearing a leotard; it just wasn't going to happen, not on her watch.

"Just going and getting human medicine isn't as easy as it once was," Rachel told her gently.

Jen felt her heart stutter. She hadn't forgotten what Cynthia had done for them, how could she? Her and Dec's child was named after the doctor, but she hadn't thought about the fact that Cynthia had been their only link to the human medical community.

"Dammit!" Jen slammed her hand down on the desk next to her. She heard Fane's growl and Decebel's answering snarl but she ignored the posturing males. They could suck it for all she cared. Her best friend was in labor; her other best friend was off goodness knows where doing whatever dirty work Peri— Jen froze as the fae's name popped into her mind. Her head whipped around to look at Vasile.

"We need a fae." She was pretty sure she looked half crazed as she stared down the Alpha, but she didn't give a damn. This was her best friend and her baby. She'd do a lot more than stare the Alpha of all Alphas in the eyes if she had to.

"I've had a little contact with Peri," Vasile admitted, "but not much, and from what I understand, the situation they are in is quite precarious."

Jen propped her hands on her hips and tried hard not to growl. She failed miserably. "I don't give a flying piece of horse poo what their situation is. Jacque needs help and Peri is the fae who can help her."

"And Peri is who will come." Alina's voice filled the room as she stepped passed a frowning Decebel.

The words had barely left Alina's mouth when the room filled with a bright light and then darkness. All of the males tensed and growls filled the darkness.

"It's good to know that nothing changes while I'm gone." Peri's voice cut through the darkness and then the light was back. The high fae stood next to the bed where Jacque lay. "You males still have no sense of humor and you females can't seem to keep your asses out of the frying pan. Alina,"—Peri bowed slightly to her—"you rang?"

"Jacque needs human medicine to keep from going into labor and popping out a furless pup and you need to get it for her," Jen said before Alina could respond. Her arms were now crossed in front of her chest as she stared down the fae.

"Well, hello to you too, Jennifer. No, no, I'm fine, please don't worry about me. And oh, Sally is doing great too. We're just having a good old time dealing with the mess Lorrelle got us into before her much too easy death."

Jen made a dismissive gesture with her hand. "I don't have time for your sister issues. You are standing on your own two feet and Costin hasn't called in the cavalry which tells me you and Sally are hanging in there. She," Jen said and motioned toward Jacque, "on the other hand, is not doing quite as well. Could we please focus on that?"

A small smile touched Peri's tight lips. "Jen, you are still just as lovely as ever. Like sitting bare assed on a cactus, you bring such joy to my life."

"Yeah and I've missed you like I miss my last yeast infection," Jen retorted.

"Like I said, it's good some things do not change. Fine, Rachel," the fae looked at the healer. "What do you need?"

Rachel's eyes were wide as she looked between Jen and Peri. "I'm not sure the name of the medicine," she said carefully, obviously worried that Jen was going to fly off the handle. "It's a drug they use to stop the contractions of labor."

"Good enough, I'm sure I can coerce some doctor to share his or her knowledge with me if you will—" Her words froze as Jen moved quickly across the room until her hand was clenched tightly around Peri's wrist. "Um,"—Peri looked at Jen as though she were a slimy bug—"what are you doing?"

"You think you're going without me? Uh, no. Besides you might need my help persuading the information out of someone."

"Or you could just look the information up on the internet," Decebel spoke up as he stepped into the room ignoring Fane's growl. "She doesn't need you to tag along, Jennifer."

Jen's eyes narrowed. "B, this is not the time. I'm going to help get Jacque what she needs. Deal with it."

"Like I said, it's good some things never change," Peri smiled.

"Good times, right?" Jen added.

"Sally and Costin don't have quite the entertainment value that you two do."

"Your own fault for not inviting me," Jen pointed out.

"True enough," Peri sighed. "But I'm here now and, as always, you have not disappointed, Jen."

"I think if we continue to sit here and talk like Dec isn't in the room seething over my lack of submission his head my pop off his neck."

Peri's faced scrunched together. "That would just be messy."

"Then, perhaps, you should—you know—" Jen made a popping motion with her hand as she said, "poof us out of her."

"I don't go poof," Peri said indignantly.

"Maybe you should; it could be more impressive then the bright lights."

Peri shrugged. "Fine, we'll poof."

Jen saw the minute Decebel realized what the pair was saying when his eyes widened and he started toward her. He was too late. She and Peri were already flashing from the room.

Jen caught her balance as she opened her eyes and saw that Peri had brought them to a hospital. She had no clue which hospital, but there was no doubt that's what it was as people in white coats walked quickly through the halls and scrub clad nurses rushed about with arms full of charts.

"I'm looking for the hospital pharmacy?" Peri's voice drew Jen's attention. She turned to see the high fae talking to one of the nurses in blue scrubs. "Yes, I've only been working here a few days and I get turned around so easily."

Jen wanted to roll her eyes. Peri was using some sort of magic over the women who was smiling back at the fae as though Peri had just shot her up with the really good pain medicine. The woman answered Peri and gave her some vague directions and then hurried on her way.

"You work here?" Jen smirked. "You have about as much right being a caregiver as I do being—"

"A stay at home stripper mom?" Peri interrupted.

Jen pursed her lips. "Ha, ha. My stripping days are over."

Peri motioned for her to follow. "Uh-hu and so if Katie Peri's E.T. suddenly started playing, you wouldn't have the sudden urge to de-robe?"

"Urge, yes," Jen admitted. "I mean, come on, the song has a sick beat. Who wouldn't have the urge when it plays?"

Peri nodded. "Good point."

They rounded several corners and took two stairwells before finally coming to a brown metal door with the word Pharmacy painted on it in white block letters. Next to it was a black square on the wall that required the scanning of a badge for entry. Peri held her hand out in front of the black square and the door made a clicking sound. The fae smiled. "Don't mind if we do," she said as she pulled the door opened and motioned Jen inside.

A short, balding man stood on the other side of a long counter. He had a round, kind face with deep set eyes and a small nose. His glasses sat perched on the edge of his nose and Jen wondered how they didn't just slip right off.

As the door shut behind them, the man's eyes looked up at them over the rim of his glasses. They widened slightly but then his surprise was replaced with what she was sure was practiced professionalism. "How can I help you ladies? Forgive me if I don't know your names. I'm rather new," he said blushing endearingly.

"Don't feel bad," Peri said good-naturedly. "We're both new too. In fact, so new that we left the chart for the patient up stairs." Peri glanced at Jen. "Do you remember the name of the drug that doctor," Peri said and glanced over Jen's shoulder, "um, Dr. Vagisile was requesting."

Jen choked back the laugh that nearly burst out at the *name* Peri had come up with. Jen's eyes narrowed. "Dr. Vagisile, the OB doctor, wanted something to help stop Ms. Cli Tauris' contractions."

Peri's eyes widened at Jen's words but Jen just turned and smiled at the pharmacist, whose face had turned a bright shade of red. Wrapped in his white lab coat, he reminded Jen of a tampon, which was just all kinds of wrong. She blamed Peri and her stupid vagsile name for that.

"Yes," Peri finally choked out. "Yes, the drug to stop Ms. Tauris' contractions."

"Oh, um, that would be, yes." The pudgy man stumbled about as he messed with something behind the counter. "The doctor is wanting…"

"He seemed to be quite in a hurry to stop them." Jen leaned forward and batted her eyes at the flustered man. "Dr. V said she was just too early to be going into labor. So we of course hurried down here to get him what he wanted as quickly as we could. Ms. Tauris looked to be in all kinds of pain with the writhing and screaming."

"Well, if you were pushing a watermelon out of your parts, you'd be writhing and screaming too," Peri pointed out. "I've heard that for a man it's comparable to them passing a kidney stone through their—"

"Terbutaline," the pharmacist blurted out. "He's wanting Terbutaline." He scurried off, his face growing redder by the second.

"I think we made him uncomfortable," Jen said as she watched him hurry to the back.

Peri shook her head. "No, we were perfectly pleasant. He probably just has to pee. We don't make people uncomfortable."

Jen laughed. "Right, and men love it when you talk about them squeezing stones through their man parts."

The high fae shrugged. "I don't see what the big deal is. We females have to squeeze small beings through our parts and nobody cringes or refrains from talking about it. Like we enjoy thinking about popping a watermelon through our who-hahs."

Jen laughed as the pudgy pharmacists came hurrying back. She patted Peri's shoulder. "Never thought I'd say this. In fact I was pretty sure I'd eat my own boob before I ever said this, but I've missed you."

Peri glanced over at Jen with a wry smile. "Awe, Jennifer, I don't get choked up often but when I'm chosen over someone eating their own boob, well, it gets me right here." She patted the place over her heart. "As much as I'm enjoying our bonding, I believe we have a patient waiting on us." She snatched the bag from the still beat-red man and took Jen's hand. They flashed right in front of the man and, based on his gasp, Peri hadn't bothered to shield him from their sudden disappearance.

When they reappeared in Fane and Jacque's room, Peri tossed the bag to Rachel but didn't give Jen time to say anything before she grabbed her again and flashed her from the room.

"What the—" Jen huffed as they appeared out in the hall and several feet away from Jacque's door. Jen's eyes widened as she saw her mate come storming out down the hall. "You know I'm about to get chewed on like his favorite squeaky toy, right?"

Peri didn't look the least bit concerned. "I might care if I didn't know that you thoroughly enjoy a good chewing."

"Jennifer," Decebel growled but was cut off by Peri.

"Save it, Alpha." Peri held up a hand and froze Decebel in midstride. "You can flap your disgruntled jaws once I'm gone. I need information." She looked back at Jen. "Has there been anything unusual happening here?"

Jen frowned. "Be a little clearer, Peri fairy. Unusual for us is sort of a staple."

"No menacing looking freaks coming around to make threats or stir mischief? No visits from the pixie king? No Great Luna bringing warnings of the end of the world?"

"Wow, sounds like you guys really are making some friends," Jen said dryly. "No, nothing like that. Jacque got herself into some trouble but it didn't have anything to do with any of that."

"Good," Peri nodded. "She made a motion with her hand that released Decebel. "Please try to stay out of trouble while we are attempting to bring order to the rest of the supernatural world. I don't have time to be poofing about rescuing your ass." And then she was gone.

"Well, she's still her usual pleasant self," Jen grumbled as she met the frustrated glare of her mate.

"Do you want to check on Jacque?" Decebel asked her in the voice that said what he really wanted to say wasn't nearly as cordial.

"You mean before you take me home and punish me for my insolence?"

"You said it, not me."

"You were thinking it."

"Touché."

Chapter 18

Jacque wasn't sure how much time had passed from the time she collapsed to the time when the pain finally began to ease. She had slipped in and out of fitful sleep brought on by Rachel's healing power. She couldn't deny that she was thankful for those moments of oblivion.

As her eyes fluttered open, the soft glow of candlelight filled her vision, along with the face of her very concerned mate.

"How are you feeling?" he asked her, regardless of the fact that he could have just looked inside of her mind himself. She appreciated that he wanted her to be the one to tell him.

"Better," she admitted. "But tired."

"You had me worried."

Jacque managed a weak smile. "That makes two of us."

They stared at each other for several long minutes before Jacque finally broached the subject she'd so diligently avoided before the crisis had hit. She knew it probably wasn't the time, but she needed to fix things.

"I'm sorry I didn't come talk to you about my worries, Fane. I'm sorry that I made a decision that involved both of us, not to mention our pack, and didn't think about how it would make you feel. I just wanted to take away your pain."

Fane brushed a finger along her jaw. His eyes roamed over her face hungrily seeming to soak all of her in. "I understand why you did it. I know what it's like to want to protect you from any and all pain and fear. I want us to be able to be honest with one another without the other feeling like they have to go to some drastic measure to fix things. Sometimes the best thing we can do for each other is just to be there. Just having you to hold, Jacquelyn, is the most soothing thing I could ask for. You are more than enough to help me get through tough times." He took a slow breath as his warm, strong hand gently encircled her throat resting across her collar bone. "I can face anything in this world with you by my side. All I ask is that you trust that. Trust that we were brought together for a reason at exactly the right moment in time. I don't think the fact that we were meant for each other is necessarily going to make anything easier, but it does make it all have more purpose."

"When did you become so wise?" Jacque asked grinning up at him. Her body shivered under his touch and she tried to keep from closing her eyes and basking in it. She realized that the scare from the labor contractions had put things into perspective for both of them.

"When I was blessed enough to have you accept me as your mate. Don't you remember? Beside every wise man is an even wiser woman."

Jacque laughed. "Now you're just trying for brownie points."

Fane shrugged. "I'll do whatever it takes to get loving from you."

"Is that what you need?" Jacque's voice dropped and warmth spread over her.

Fane's eyes began to glow. "I want nothing more than to hold you, skin to skin, but Rachel has forbid any form of physical intimacy. She said we needed to make sure the medicine is going to keep your contractions at bay. So you are officially on bed rest."

"Well, that's a bummer." Jacque tapped her chin. "I guess you will just have to entertain me."

He quirked an eyebrow at her. "Oh? And how am I to do that, Luna?"

Jacque didn't even blush when she answered. "I think a strip show by my fine specimen of a husband is in order. Even if we can't physically be together, that doesn't mean I can't enjoy the view."

Fane threw his head back and laughed as he sat up and pulled his shirt over his head revealing his very toned torso. "If a view is what my female wants, then that is what she will get."

Jacque looked at his exquisite form taking in her fill. He really was something to look at.

"You're turn," Fane told her with a smoldering look that she was sure would melt steel.

Her eyes widened. "You want me to take off my shirt?"

He shook his head. "All of it. Like you said, I can look, just not touch."

He reached for her but she held up a hand. "Wait one sec, Casanova. Before I bare all for you, are you okay? Like with everything?"

Fane laid a hand on her hip tugging her toward him. "It's getting better. Seeing you in that much pain, and also seeing what could have been, has helped me let go of a lot of my fears. I'm not saying I'm not still scared of somethings but I think a lot of that is natural. After all, we are young and being a parent is a scary, intimidating thing. But like I said, together we can do this."

Jacque felt her eyes fill with tears. "We're going to be okay, right?"

"Beloved, we are so much better than okay." He tugged at the hem of her shirt and helped her pull it over her head. "And we are about to be even better than that." He laid down next to her and pulled her body close against his letting his warmth absorb into her. Their chest pressed together and their hearts pounded out a steady rhythm seeming to say with every beat that they were exactly where they were supposed to be—together, complete, whole.

Decebel held Jennifer in his arms as they sat on the floor in front of the burning fire. It was finally getting cool enough to have a fire again, and the warm flames danced sensually across his mate's skin.

"You think we are all going to be okay?" Jennifer asked as she pressed her face against his bare chest.

"What do you mean?"

"Sally is off doing who knows what with Peri and all those new healers. I mean, what is up with all those chicks suddenly appearing? Healers are a big deal and you know every pack without one is going to be clamoring to get their grubby paws on one. That can't be good for unity purposes. And then there's Jacque and Fane and all their crap plus the worry of her losing the baby. And then there's us."

"What about us?" Decebel frowned down at her. "I thought we were fine. We had our fight, we made up, with incredible love making I might add, and I'm planning to make sure you stay too tired to cause any more problems."

"I'm going to pretend you didn't just say that I cause problems. Because what I know you meant was that I bring you such joy you can barely contain yourself and you struggle with the urge not to run to the top of the mountains singing 'the hills are alive with the sound of music.'" Her voice echoed around the room as she sang out the last part.

"Okay so, perhaps, we *should* be worrying about us. And if I ever do perform such a feminine act please kick me in my man parts."

Jennifer patted his leg. "Consider it done, baby."

Decebel ran his hand down her long hair enjoying the way the silk strands felt against his skin. His mind flashed back to earlier and the feel of her hair on his face and chest and her scent surrounding him. She was definitely a handful, but she was his.

"In answer to your question," he said quietly not wanting to disturb their peaceful moment, "we are all going to be fine. We've already made it through some tough times. We just have to stay united not only as mates and partners but as pack as well. Evil will seek to divide us to weaken us, and we at times will even try to sabotage ourselves in our misguided efforts to fix things that are beyond our control, but if we stand beside one another, support one another, and love each other, we will persevere. As for us, you're stuck with me, babe. Where you go, I go."

"To hell and back?" Jennifer asked and he heard the teasing in her voice.

But in his answer there was no jesting. He meant it with every cell in his body. "To hell and back as many times as you need me to go."

She pulled back and looked up at him. "That's all I need to know." She leaned up and pressed a kiss to his lips, and Decebel felt all of her worries fade away as she once again gave herself to him. As always, his mate was generous with herself and her affection and Decebel reveled in her attention. He had no doubt that their time of peace would soon be coming to an end. His wolf sensed it and was growing restless. But for now, he would push the worries away and find peace and comfort in his mate's arms.

Chapter 19

Lilly watched as the king of the warlocks paced the main hall in the mountain they called home. She was still growing use to living in such a grand and old fashioned place, but it was beginning to feel like home. She and Cypher had yet to say any formal vows, and though they shared a bed, because her warlock refused to leave, their relationship had not progressed physically. If things continued they way they had been recently, she wondered if they'd ever get around to getting married. Lilly knew she shouldn't be worried about that, and she wasn't, not really. But the little girl in her who dreamed of the white dress couldn't help but hope that, even at over forty years of age, it would happen soon.

"Are you going to talk with Vasile about it?" She finally broke the silence that had been between them since she'd returned from seeing her daughter. When Lilly had gotten back she'd found Cypher and his top council members in deep discussion over the continuing decline of their people. Every day another warlock fell victim to the madness that seemed to be claiming them.

Cypher was getting desperate to help them. And yet she knew that he honestly didn't have any idea how to fix the problem. The magic in the human realm had grown weak, and it almost seemed as if the warlocks were beginning to soak up all of the evil that had been left over, like a residue, across their mountain over the years.

"I understand your ties to the wolves because of your daughter, Lilly, but it isn't in our nature to seek out help when it will reveal a weakness about ourselves."

He'd told her that already in many different ways, but she still didn't agree. "Will you let pride be your downfall then?"

His yellow eyes narrowed. "It isn't pride to want to protect my people."

"Vasile and his wolves have come to your aide before and they did not exploit your weaknesses then. Why do you think they would suddenly do so now? When are you going to see that you aren't god. You can't fix everything on your own. It is okay to need help." Lilly was pleading with him again. She had yet to admit to him that she was terrified she was going to lose him to the madness that had taken others. She couldn't stand the thought of her strong, powerful warlock king reduced to animal like behavior and unable to be the leader he was born to be. She needed him and whether he realized it or not, he needed her.

"I'm not going to keep arguing with you about this, Lilly," he said sounding every bit as tired as he looked.

"Are you plannng on sending me away again?"

His head snapped up. "No, I told you I wouldn't do that again."

"Then I guess you will argue with me about it as many times as I bring it up. I am not one of your subjects and I will not turn a blind eye while you run foolishly into a battle you can't win on your own. That is what a partner is, Cypher—someone to help you see what you can't, and to challenge you, and to question you so that you look at all the possibilities."

"Perhaps, I have been alone in my duties for too long and I cannot change," he rumbled as he turned to face the large throne that sat at the front of the hall. It looked cold and lonely up there but it was no longer by itself. Next to it now sat a smaller more feminine throne—one she had not sat on yet because she didn't feel right doing so, as she wasn't yet his bride. It aggravated him to no end, which really was just a bonus.

"You can believe your excuses if you want but I'm not interested in what you're selling. If you want me, then you will fight for me—for us. If you want your people to be well again, then you will fight for them, and you will take on any help you can in order to be victorious. So don't try and spout that *I'm too old to change* crap to me. I've been single for eighteen years and yet I'm willing to let go of some control in order to have happiness with you. You have to meet me half way."

Cypher stared at her with frustration marring his handsome face. It wasn't a new argument and Lilly wasn't foolish enough to believe that they wouldn't have it again and again, but it was one worth fighting. She would not accept laziness in their relationship. It would take hard work on both of their parts to be successful, but she wanted it and she believed he did too. Now she just had to figure out how to help him save his people and possibly himself.

"We can do this, Cypher." She took a step toward him, and another, until she stood directly in front of him. She reached up to his face and placed her palm on his skin. Cypher leaned into her hand making her insides tingle with desire. "You are worth it to me. Am I to you?"

His large arms circled her waist and pulled her tightly against him. He leaned down and pressed his forehead to hers and let out a long, deep breath. "You are worth more than you know, Little One. I know I am difficult and unbending but I will fight for you. Whatever it takes, you are mine."

"Then we will do this together. We will save your people."

"Our people," he corrected before pressing his lips to hers.

Our people, Lilly thought to herself as she let Cypher's love wrap around her. He was right; she had to begin to see them as her people even though she was human. If she loved Cypher and would do anything she could for him, she had to love them just as she did him. She had to be willing to go all in and build a life with him. Jacque was moving forward in her own life, married and now with a child on the way, and it was time for

Lilly to move forward with hers. Never in a million years would she have thought it would be at the side of a warlock king, but as he pulled her tighter against him, his hands moving lower on her lower back and his lips devouring hers, she realized that there was no place else on earth that she belonged like she did there with him.

From the author:

I hope you enjoyed getting to see how Fane and Jacque are doing while they prepare for the birth of their child. Stay tuned for the next Grey Wolves Series Novella, Queen of the Warlocks, where we will embark on a harrowing journey with Lilly and Cypher to save their people.

Books by Quinn

Grey Wolves Series
Prince of Wolves
Blood Rites
Just One Drop
Out of the Dar
Beyond the Veil
Fate and Fury
Sacrifice of Love
Luna of Mine

Grey Wolves Novella's
Piercing Silence
Queen of the Warlocks (Coming soon)

Gypsy Healers Series
Into the Fae
Wolf of Stone

Elfin Series
Elfin
Rapture
Surrender (Coming soon)

Dream Makers Series
Dream of Me
Dream so Dark (Coming soon)

Stand Alone Works
Call Me Crazy

Printed in Great Brit.
by Amazon